THE PREGNANT AMISH WIDOW

EXPECTANT AMISH WIDOWS BOOK 2

SAMANTHA PRICE

CHAPTER 1

Therefore if any man be in Christ, he is a new creature:
old things are passed away;
behold, all things are become new.
2 Corinthians 5:17

"ARE you sure you want to do this?"

Grace was jolted out of her daydreams. The rhythmic clip-clopping of the horse pulling her brother's buggy had brought back memories of bygone years. Life was simpler back then. Being the youngest of eleven children, and the only girl, she'd always been coddled and protected when she was growing up.

Grace answered her brother. "Yes. I need to do it or else I don't know what will happen to me." Newly widowed, Grace Stevens was heading to the bishop's house to talk with him about returning to her Amish roots and being baptized. She knew she had to turn away from the *Englisch* life she'd been living with her late husband, Jeremy, and make a decision about her life so she could move forward.

"If you get baptized, it'll be forever, and if you return to live life as an *Englischer* you'll be shunned. Wouldn't it be better to wait a few days and see how you feel then? With the shock of Jeremy's death and everything, you might not be thinking straight." Taking his eyes off the road for a moment, Matthew glanced over at her.

She forced a smile and put on a brave front as she was so used to doing. "I have to do this. I've had a lot of time to think about it." In fact, she'd had four long years to think about it. For those years, she'd been married to an outsider, an *Englischer.* She'd moved right into his apartment after leaving the community. The first few months together had been fine, but after they had married Jeremy became like Jekyll and Hyde – and she was never to recognize the warning signs of his mood swings. One minute he'd be attentive and sweet, and then she'd do or say something that would send him into the opposite mood. He'd been abusive in every way possible – mentally, physically, and emotionally – but she'd stayed because she believed marriage was forever. Besides, when her marriage had been good, it had been wonderful.

Finally she'd had enough of his seesaw moods and

walking on eggshells, and she'd told him she was through. Two days later Jeremy was dead. She couldn't help but think that if she hadn't said she was leaving, he'd still be alive. While the counselor her doctor had recommended made her see that Jeremy's death wasn't her fault, she still struggled with it. She repeated daily what the counselor had told her. *Jeremy made his own decisions.*

Grace put her fingertips against the faint bruises, which were the result of Jeremy trying to choke her on that last day. She'd told him she'd had enough of him and their marriage. He'd gone into a rage, put his hands around her throat and choked her. While she was lying on the floor gasping for air, she heard his car zoom away. That was the last time she saw him.

Grace had scraped herself off the floor, packed her things and booked into a nearby hotel. She figured she'd give him a day to calm down, and then she hoped he'd be civil enough that they could discuss what to do with the apartment they'd been leasing. When she saw he hadn't been home for two days, she became worried and reported him as a missing person. It was then that she found out he was in the morgue as a John Doe. She was told he'd been drinking at a bar and had then driven off a bridge, intoxicated. Suicide? Grace would never know if it had been a deliberate act or an accident. If she hadn't threatened to leave, he might still be alive today. Now she'd have to live with the guilt of his death every day of her life. His family thought she was to blame, and none of them talked to her at his funeral.

Matthew glanced over at her. "What's wrong?"

"Nothing."

"I know that look. Apart from your mouth being turned down at the corners, you keep sighing. Tell me what's wrong."

"I'm just thinking what a mess I've made of my life."

"We all make mistakes. It's how we deal with them that's important."

Grace nodded. Her brother was right in a general sense, but he'd never be able to understand the horrors and the torment she'd lived through. How would anyone be able to recognize how she felt unless they'd experienced abuse first-hand?

"I'm concerned you're being baptized so quickly because of the shock of everything that's just happened. I suppose I shouldn't say things about Jeremy because he's gone now, but from the bits and pieces you've told me you've been through a few rough years."

"There were good times. When they were good, they were very, very good." Jeremy had kept her isolated, and hadn't allowed her to have her own friends. As she'd had no one in whom she could confide, she'd become an expert at keeping things to herself. She'd told Matthew some things, but not everything - she was too embarrassed, and besides that, she couldn't shake the nagging feeling that it had all been her fault.

Grace giggled to make light of his words and to hide her pain. "It sounds like you don't want me to be baptized."

He frowned and glanced over at her again. "Of course, I do. You know that I do. It's just that I want you to join for the right reasons and not because you had a terrible time of it after you left. Why don't you give yourself some time? There's no hurry."

"Please stop, Matthew! I've decided to do it, and that's that."

Matthew leaned back in his seat and kept quiet.

Grace closed her eyes, tried to empty her mind, and enjoyed the sound of the horse and buggy as they made their way down the winding ribbon-like roads toward Bishop Micah's house.

She'd had years to work out what was right for her life. All she wanted was to be baptized and do the right thing in *Gott's* sight. She'd had too many years without Him in her life. It annoyed her that Jeremy had never allowed her to see her *familye*, and she'd allowed him to control her.

Grace opened her eyes. "I'm sorry I didn't go to your wedding. I wanted to."

Matthew chuckled. "That was some time ago. You don't have to be sorry for anything. I would hope that you will try and get on better with Marlene since we're all living in the same *haus*."

Matthew and Marlene had been living with Grace and Matthew's parents since they'd gotten married while they saved for a home of their own.

"I'll try to get along with her."

Matthew looked over at her and studied her face. "You know, Marlene's quite willing to get along with you, and she has no idea why you don't like her."

She couldn't tell Matthew what she thought of Marlene, and neither could she tell him what Marlene had done to her a few years back. He'd always looked at the trouble-making Marlene through rose-colored glasses. She and Marlene had been the best of friends until Marlene had ruined things for her with Adam, the boy Grace had been in love with.

Grace had been dating Adam for six months, but Marlene noticed Jeremy was always hanging around the coffee shop where both she and Grace worked. Although she'd given him no encouragement or reason to continue his interest in her, Jeremy had asked Grace out several times. Marlene had opened her big mouth to Adam and made it sound like Grace was meeting Jeremy in secret. Adam had chosen to believe Marlene and Adam ended their relationship. When she'd learned what Marlene had said, Grace had been distraught. Jeremy had been there at the right time to provide a shoulder to cry on, and their relationship had developed quickly from there.

At the time, Grace had been certain that Marlene had wanted Adam for herself, but Marlene had switched her focus to Matthew. Had Marlene married Matthew just to annoy her? It certainly seemed so to Grace.

Now her refuge and the only place Grace felt safe, also housed Marlene, the girl who'd set her life off-course. "How long do you think you and Marlene will be staying at *Mamm* and *Dat's haus?*"

Matthew tipped his hat back and scratched his head in an agitated manner. "At the slow rate we're saving money, I'd say it'll be another two years before we can scrape together a decent deposit."

Grace knew that Matthew was annoyed that Marlene refused to get a job to help them save for a home of their own. Even a part-time job would've helped.

Everything about Marlene annoyed Grace since they'd fallen out - her pale round face, the smattering of freckles on her cheeks, and her strawberry-blonde hair that always found its way out of the sides of her prayer *kapp.* If Grace was going to commit her life to God, she knew she'd have to tolerate Marlene as one of God's children and see past her annoyance with her.

"I'm afraid you're stuck with me and Marlene for a while, Grace."

Grace gave a laugh. "It takes *Mamm* and *Dat's* attention away from me. I know *Dat* wants to say 'I told you so' about me marrying Jeremy. *Mamm's* probably thinking the same thing."

Jeremy had been a liar and a cheat. She'd found out

much later that even on their honeymoon he'd been receiving texts from other women. He'd admitted to being unfaithful and had promised to change, but he never had. Grace had never shared the fact that he'd been unfaithful; she was too embarrassed.

"Not long to go now," Matthew said.

She wondered what the bishop was going to ask her, or whether he'd ask her anything at all. Perhaps she was supposed to give him reasons why she wanted to return.

Grace was grateful that Matthew had been quiet most of their drive, giving her time to collect her thoughts. She'd made the decision when she married Jeremy that she would remain away from the Amish. To return four years later seemed as though she was going backward in her life rather than forward.

When the bishop's house came into view, she took a deep breath. She knew she was doing the right thing to get her life into order - taking a step back was the only way she knew to move forward.

CHAPTER 2

For I know the thoughts that I think toward you, saith the
LORD, thoughts of peace,
and not of evil, to give you an expected end.
Jeremiah 29:11

GRACE SMOOTHED HER SHORT, cropped hair back under her prayer *kapp*. She'd rather the bishop not see that her hair had been cut. Jeremy had made her cut her thigh-length hair because he liked it short and spiked. Now that she was back in the community, her hair was just another reminder of how far she'd moved away from her faith.

"You okay?" her brother asked.

"*Jah.* I need to sit for a while before I go in." She looked at the bishop's house and knew she didn't have much longer before the bishop or his wife came out to greet them. Their house was a modest home and small in size for one in which twelve children had been raised. The bishop's children were now grown, leaving Bishop Micah and his wife, Helga, on their own.

Matthew gave her a big smile and put a comforting hand on her shoulder. "Do you want me to come in with you? I'd rather wait here, but I'll come in with you if you want."

She'd always felt better with her big brother around. She'd missed the close family bonds and the friendliness of the community, and that was one thing she knew she'd appreciate about being back. Grace grabbed her brother's hand. "You'll be waiting here? You won't go anywhere?"

"I'll sit right here. Go on; you'll be okay."

"I know it." Grace had always been nervous whenever she'd talked to Bishop Micah. She always felt as though she never measured up to his expectations.

Grace jumped down from the buggy. As she walked, she listened to the crunching sounds that her feet made against the loose pebbles on the path that led to the porch. Before she knocked on the door, she turned around to get another look at her brother's reassuring face. He gave her a nod, and as she turned back to knock, the door swung open. In front of her stood Bishop Micah. His dark beard was longer, but apart from that he looked just the same. He grasped her hand and pulled her into his small home.

"Grace, I was so pleased to hear from your *vadder* that you wanted to be baptized."

Grace found herself relaxing thanks to his friendly manner. Before she had a chance to respond to what he'd said, Helga hurried toward her.

"Grace, it's so *gut* to see you again. Come and sit down in the living room. I've made us tea and cookies."

Unlike her husband, Helga had changed. She'd put on a great deal of weight, which had made her face fuller but hadn't detracted from her attractiveness. Being with Jeremy for so long had made Grace more focused on people's physical appearance.

She sat on the couch still not knowing what to expect. Would the bishop ask her difficult questions and ask why she wanted to be baptized after all this time? Or would it be a more relaxed, informal occasion since there were tea and cookies?

Helga passed Grace a cup of tea after she handed one to her husband.

Grace took a sip of tea from the white china cup, and then plunged right into the reason she was there. She looked at the bishop. "Did my *vadder* tell you I want to be baptized?" She remembered the bishop had just told her that so she added, "He didn't exactly say what he said, but I do want to join the community properly. I've lived as an *Englischer* and decided it's not for me."

The bishop had just taken a mouthful of tea. He swallowed and then placed the teacup back onto the saucer. He nodded, and then looked directly into her eyes. "Your *vadder* told me what happened to your husband a few weeks back. Helga and I are deeply sorry that your husband passed without knowing *Gott's* salvation."

Grace hung her head and looked down into her tea. Jeremy had always teased her about growing up Amish even though he hadn't seemed to mind when they'd first met. He'd taunted her about it in their many arguments. She tilted her head upward. "He's gone now, and I want to put my past life behind me so I can move forward."

"We cannot be unequally yoked with unbelievers. It never works out."

Grace looked into the bishop's sympathetic face. "I know."

The bishop grinned widely. "The old things are passed away, and all things become new. When you're baptized, you're a new creature in *Gott's* sight. All your sins are washed away."

In her mind, Grace could hear Jeremy laughing at the bishop. She could even hear him laughing at Helga and cruelly mocking the size of her. Grace nodded at the bishop and then sipped her tea some more. She wanted to be rid of Jeremy and all reminders of him. "That's exactly what I want. I want to be a new creature and to be born again. I need a new start." That was one thing she knew Jeremy would hate for her to say.

"That's good, Grace," Helga said while passing her a plate of cookies.

Grace looked down at the plate before her. Instead of seeing cookies, she saw a pile of white sugar and white flour, all of which she hadn't touched in years to retain her slim figure. Jeremy had demanded that she stay skinny, and she'd done her best to please him. She smiled as she reached for one of the sugar-laden treats. *"Denke,* Helga." Grace took the largest cookie on the plate.

"You understand the seriousness of the commitment you're about to undertake?" The bishop leaned forward and his eyes seemed to bore through to her soul.

Grace chewed her mouthful quickly so she could answer. She swallowed before she had properly chewed and it stuck in her throat. Putting her hand to her neck, she started coughing. Helga flew off her chair, ran into the kitchen, and brought back a glass of water. Grace took mouthfuls to wash the cookie crumbs down. She was certain she could hear Jeremy laughing at the scene she'd just created.

"Denke, Helga." Grace placed the glass on the coffee table in front of her and then nibbled some more on the delicious cookie. She'd forgotten how good sugar tasted.

"All better now?" Helga asked.

When Grace nodded, Helga sat down.

Grace rubbed at the sides of her temples with her

fingertips. The bishop had just asked her a question before she choked. She looked into the bishop's concerned face. *"Jah.* I do understand the seriousness of everything, and I'm ready for it. I've lived as an *Englischer,* and I want nothing more than to come back home to the community, be baptized, and enjoy *Gott's* kingdom."

Without blinking the bishop asked, "Do you hold any bitterness in your heart against anyone?"

She did, but how did he know? Or was that something he asked of everyone?

"Doesn't all that get washed away when we're baptized?" Grace asked.

"Once you become a believer, all your sins are washed away, but it's up to us to keep sin away from the heart. A root of bitterness can grow and pull your heart away from *Gott."*

Has Dat told the bishop that Marlene and I don't get along? If so, then why aren't they talking to Marlene like this? Grace bit her lip. Then there was Jeremy. How would she ever forgive Jeremy for all the things he did to her? Grace took a deep breath.

"Is there anything you want to talk to me about?" he asked.

Would the bishop say that she had to forgive Jeremy before she could get baptized? She didn't know if she could ever find it in her heart to forgive him, but she *did* want to be baptized.

Grace felt tears stinging behind her eyes. Wasn't she

14

better to bury feelings about Jeremy rather than speaking about them? She thought it best to come clean. "It's just that I don't think I can ever forgive Jeremy for all the horrible things he did to me." Grace hung her head. Out of the corner of her eye, she saw the bishop and his wife look at each other.

"None of us is perfect, Grace. We walk a daily walk and do the best we can. Jeremy didn't have the advantage of knowing *Gott* like you do," he said.

Grace looked up. The bishop's words were true. Jeremy had gotten furious whenever she'd mentioned God. Even though she took into consideration what the bishop said, she still hated Jeremy and knew it would take a long time for her broken heart to heal. He'd ruined her life. "I'm willing to work on my feelings toward him."

"We forgive others because He first forgave us."

Despite the image in her head of Jeremy doubled over laughing at the bishop, Grace nodded once more at what he had just said. "That makes sense."

"Not everything will make sense. And when things don't, we accept what He says by faith. For by grace are we saved and that is *Gott's* gift to us."

"So when can I be baptized?"

"We've got a few others who'll be doing the required Bible studies and receiving the instructions. Monday night, right here, at seven in the evening; you can come here for the Bible study."

"So in a few weeks?" Grace asked.

"*Nee,* this very next Monday, and then the next few Mondays after that. I don't know how long it will take to get through it all; it varies depending on the amount of questions people have."

"So you've not got long to wait, Grace," Helga said while offering her another cookie.

She took one. "I'm looking forward to my new life." Grace had always had a sweet tooth. It hadn't been easy for her to stay off candy, chocolate, and especially ice cream. She didn't have to worry about her weight now that she was no longer under Jeremy's control. He would often pinch her hips and make nasty comments. Now if she got fat, no one would notice under her roomy Amish dresses.

After another cup of tea and two more cookies, the visit with the bishop and his wife had come to a close. They walked Grace to the door.

"That's not Matthew out there waiting for you, is it?" Helga asked, looking at his buggy.

"*Jah.* He didn't want to intrude on our conversation, so he waited for me in the buggy."

"What a good *bruder,*" Bishop Micah said.

"He always has been." Grace said goodbye to the couple and headed toward the buggy.

Matthew waved at Helga and Bishop Micah, and they waved back.

When Grace climbed into the buggy, she said, "That talk made me feel much better."

THE PREGNANT AMISH WIDOW

"Gut. I'm glad." Matthew waved again at the bishop and his wife who stood in their doorway.

The bishop called out, "Monday night, Grace, don't forget."

"I'll be there," she called back. She turned to Matthew. "I'll be baptized in a few weeks. I've got a Bible study every Monday night."

"I'll drive you there. *Mamm* and *Dat* will be pleased."

And Marlene? Grace wondered. *"Denke* for driving me out here today, Matthew. I know this is right for me. I know you've had your doubts, but it's something I'm ready for."

He glanced over at her. "That means our whole *familye* has stayed in the community. All eleven of us."

"I suppose that is a rare thing these days." As they drove back home, Grace wondered where she'd be now if Marlene hadn't ruined things with Adam all those years ago. She'd most likely be happily married to him with two, or even three children by now. She'd been back home for days, but no one had mentioned Adam even though he lived on the next-door property. It was most peculiar. Her mother had given her updates on nearly everyone else in the community but hadn't said a word about him, and Grace had been too scared to ask. She had to assume that Adam had been married sometime in those four years she'd been away.

CHAPTER 3

My little children, let us not love in word, neither in tongue;
but in deed and in truth.
1 John 3:18

WHEN GRACE ARRIVED back home from her visit to the bishop's house, she walked into the kitchen to see her mother putting up preserves while Marlene was nowhere to be seen.

"*Mamm,* you should've waited for me to help you with all of this."

"Nonsense. Anyway, I've become used to doing things on my own ever since you left."

"What about Marlene?"

Matthew had just walked into the house through

the back door and had overheard her comment. "Remember what we talked about, Grace?"

"Well, shouldn't she be helping *Mamm?* What's her excuse this time?"

"If you must know, Grace, I'm not feeling well today."

Grace swung around to see that Marlene had just entered the kitchen behind her.

"I was just wondering where you were," Grace said. "Do you feel better now?"

"Not that you would care, but I've come down now to help *Mamm* with the preserves even though I still don't feel well."

Since Grace had arrived home, it had grated on her nerves to hear her sister-in-law call her mother and father *Mamm* and *Dat.*

"Marlene and I can do this on our own, Grace. Why don't you go and take a nice walk? It won't be long before it's too cold to go out, and it's such a lovely day."

Grace knew from the look on her mother's face that she was trying to keep the two girls apart. "Okay. If you're sure you don't need my help?"

"We're fine," Marlene said. "*Mamm* and I can handle it. This kitchen is too small for three."

Grace walked out of the house convinced that Marlene was trying her best to continue ruining her life. Her thoughts turned again to Adam Stoll from next door. She strolled down to the creek on his property until she sat at the bank under a spreading tree that, at one time, had been their special place. Years ago, Adam had carved their initials in that tree. She walked around the tree until she found it. It was still there, their initials surrounded by a heart. Peace and contentment filled her heart as she reached up and traced the carving with her fingertips. Maybe if she closed her eyes tightly and wished very hard, time would go back five years. If only!

She closed her eyes and imagined those lazy summer days in the fields - the feel of the sun on her skin, the smell of fresh hay, and the sight of blue and yellow wildflowers scattered here and there.

A wave of nausea clutched at Grace's stomach and she knew she was going to be sick. She left the tree and walked around, hoping that would rid her of the nausea. She should have known better than to eat all those cookies at the bishop's house in one go. Her stomach wasn't used to all that processed food. As soon as she thought about those cookies, she leaned against the nearest tree and was sick. She heaved up not just once, but three times.

As she leaned against the tree, trying to figure out whether she might be sick again, out of the corner of her eye she noticed something move. She focused her eyes and saw Adam hurrying toward her.

"Grace, are you all right?"

Could there be a worse time for Adam to see her? Life seemed to be working against her.

When he came closer, she shook her head too nauseous to speak.

"What can I get you? Water? You stay here. I'll go back to the house to get you some."

She nodded, trying not to look at him, or let him get a good look at her since she most likely had sick all over her face. When he disappeared in the direction of the house, she stepped down to the stream and washed her face in the cold water before walking back to where she'd been.

In no time, Adam was back with a large glass of water. "Here rinse your mouth," he ordered.

She took the glass and rinsed, and then spat, a couple of times. This was not the way she'd envisioned their reunion to be. It wouldn't matter if he was now married, but what if he was still single?

"Better?"

She nodded, and then put the glass into his outstretched hand.

"Come here," he ordered placing his coat on the ground so she could sit on it.

She sat on his coat and he sat next to her.

"What's made you sick?"

"I was at the bishop's house and ate too many cookies. I haven't eaten sugar or white flour for about four years. I shouldn't have eaten so many." She shook her head and looked away from him feeling like a fool.

"Have you developed food intolerances?"

She was too embarrassed to tell him that Jeremy

demanded she stay pencil-thin. *"Nee.* I just ate too much I think."

"I hear that you're back for good, and you're getting baptized soon."

Grace smiled. "How have you learned that? I've only just found that out myself."

Adam laughed. "I just saw Matthew and he told me."

"I must have been sitting down here at the creek for longer than I thought. He was just at the *haus* when I left."

It seemed nothing had changed; Matthew and Adam had been best friends since they were boys.

"I heard about what happened to your husband. I'm very sorry."

"Denke, Adam."

She wanted to tell him the truth of everything that had happened, but nothing she could tell him would improve the way he saw her now, thanks to Marlene. If she told him she'd been about to leave Jeremy two days before he died, he'd think less of her for giving up on her marriage. Maybe he too would think she was the cause of his death, just as Jeremy's family believed.

She looked into Adam's handsome face and knew that he thought that she had just lost the love of her life. The truth was she hadn't. Adam had been the love of her life, and she still didn't know if he'd gotten married.

He stared back at her. "I'm glad you're back. Nothing has been the same around here since you left."

With those soft words and the way he looked at her, she knew in her heart that he hadn't married. "What's happened with you in the last few years? You still living at your parents' *haus?*"

"Haven't you heard?"

She held her breath and braced herself for him to say that he'd gotten married. She shook her head. "Heard what?"

"Two years ago, my parents got pneumonia and went home to be with *Gott.* First *Dat,* and then two days later *Mamm.*"

Grace's fingertips flew to her mouth as she gasped. "Both of them?"

He nodded. "I live in the house alone now." Adam had been an only child, which was rare in their community where most couples had between five and twelve children.

"That's such a shock. I've only been home a few days. I'm still catching up on everything that's gone on in the community - that's why I didn't know about your parents. I wish someone would've said something. I should've kept in contact."

She could see Adam's body stiffen. "You can't concern yourself with things from the past that you can't change."

Grace took a deep breath and nodded. She wanted to keep in touch, but Jeremy had not allowed it, and she had been fearful of his temper and also desperate to please him. "You're not married, then,

Adam?" She knew already by him saying he lived alone that he wasn't, but if he was close to being married he should tell her now.

His body relaxed again, and he smiled. "No, I'm not. Did I mention I'm glad you're back?"

"It wasn't the best way to see me. Being sick, I mean." Grace felt her face flush scarlet, and she had to look away.

"That doesn't bother me. I'm just happy you're back."

"I'm glad to be back as well. I missed my *familye.* It's good to be back where I belong."

"So this is where you are!"

Adam and Grace turned their heads to see who belonged to the cranky female voice. It was Marlene.

CHAPTER 4

Not rendering evil for evil, or railing for railing: but contrariwise blessing; knowing that ye are thereunto called, that ye should inherit a blessing.

1 Peter 3:9

"WHY DO you seem so surprised, Marlene? *Mamm* told me that I should go for a walk."

Marlene placed her hands on her hips and narrowed her eyes. "It would be just like you to disappear when there's work to be done."

She was doing it again, but this time Grace was determined not to let her get away with anything. "That's not so, Marlene, and you know it. You told me there was only room for two in the kitchen, and you said that you and *Mamm* were fine."

"Grace, I told you I was feeling unwell. Couldn't you have been a little more caring?"

Grace wanted to groan. How could she answer without sounding like a mean person in front of Adam? Marlene would've known that Adam wanted a decent, hard-working woman as a wife and now she was making out that Grace was lazy.

To Grace's surprise, Adam leaned over and touched Grace on her shoulder. "Grace is not feeling well."

Marlene's mouth fell open. "I'm the one who's sick. I told her that back at the *haus.*"

"Will you give us a moment, Marlene? We were having a private discussion. When you get back home, tell your *mudder*-in-law that Grace won't be long."

Marlene looked as if she were about to say something, but instead, she turned and stomped away.

"I hope you feel better soon," Adam called after her. He waited until Marlene was farther away before he spoke to Grace again. "Don't worry; I know what she's like. It took me a while but eventually I figured it out." He laughed. "It didn't take me that long, but when I realized she'd been lying about you and the *Englischer,* it was too late - you'd already left the community. I tried to find you and that was when I found out you were already living with him. I was a little surprised that you moved so fast."

"You found out she'd been lying?"

He nodded.

"I can't believe how stupid I've been. I acted too

hastily. I was young and stupid and didn't think things through. You must think I'm a fool."

He raised his eyebrows. "Impulsive is the word I'd use. I hoped you'd come back one day. I never thought it would be under these circumstances. And I don't think you're a fool."

He held out his hands. When she put her hands in his, he pulled her to her feet. "Come on. I'll walk you back to the *haus* so Marlene can't tell your *mudder* some large stories about what we were doing out here."

"Don't you mean tall tales?"

"Those too," he said with a laugh.

When Grace's house came into view, Adam said, "Will you forgive me for believing Marlene? I've felt bad about that for so long." He put his hand on his heart. "Even though my feelings toward you were strong, I listened to what Marlene had said, and it was dumb of me."

"Let's put that behind us. I'm just glad that you know now that she made the whole thing up. Jeremy had made advances toward me, but I never responded, not once. I told him I had a man in my life already. When things with you were over, I agreed to go on a date with him. I guess it felt good that someone wanted my company and was giving me the attention that I wished you were giving me." She was glad that she finally had the chance to explain things to him. It was one burden lifted off her shoulders.

Adam nodded. "I can see how it would've happened,

and I don't blame Marlene. She was young at the time and immature. I guess we all were back then."

"That's true." *Yes, that's true, but you didn't run away and marry someone totally unsuitable. And Marlene made a good marriage with my brother.*

He stopped and touched her arm slightly, so she stopped too.

"I know this might be too soon for you, Grace, right after your husband has gone, but do you think I might be able to see you again sometime soon? Just you and me?"

Grace's heart pumped hard against her chest. "I'd like that." Those were the only words she could manage.

His concerned face relaxed into a smile as he placed a hand on the small of her back while they walked forward.

When they arrived at the house, Grace's mother raced out to meet Adam. "Come in, Adam. Marlene said you were with Grace. Come on in and I'll make you that strong coffee you like."

"Denke, Mrs. Byler, but I really do need to get back."

"Nonsense; come inside. We're due for a break, and we can have a nice talk about things."

"Any other time I would, but I'm expecting someone back at the *haus."*

Mrs. Byler's brow furrowed. "How about you join us for the evening meal, then?"

"Tonight?"

"Jah, tonight."

"I'd love to."

Grace stood next to her mother and watched Adam walk away. Once he was gone, her mother went upstairs while Grace went to the kitchen. Grace rolled up her sleeves ready to wash the dishes when Marlene came up beside her.

"No one will think it's right if you start making eyes at him after your husband has just died."

She turned and looked into Marlene's glinting green eyes. For once in her life, Marlene might have been right, and from the look on her face, she knew it.

With her chin tilted in the air, Marlene continued, "No one would be better for you than Adam, and you've got a second chance now that Jeremy's out of the picture."

"If things are meant to happen between us they will." Grace filled up the sink with hot water and squeezed a little soap from the dispenser.

"You're not going to make a move on him?"

Grace frowned at her sister-in-law. "You just told me everyone would think it too soon."

"Mamm doesn't believe so. She couldn't wait for him to come to dinner tonight."

"He often used to come for dinner."

"I can't wait to see what happens tonight."

Grace turned the tap off and plunged her hands into the sudsy water. "Please don't embarrass me in front of everyone."

"It'll only be our *familye* and Adam."

Grace's mother stuck her head into the kitchen. "I hope you girls aren't arguing again."

"*Nee, Mamm.* I was just trying to talk Grace into making some shoofly pies to impress Adam."

"*Jah, gut* idea, Marlene."

"*Mamm!*" Grace turned to look at her mother.

"I said the shoofly pies were a *gut* idea. We haven't had them in ages. That's all I meant," her mother said, moving further into the kitchen.

"Oh." Grace turned back to the dishes.

"I know you like him, Grace, but don't you think that if something were going to happen, it would've already?" Marlene asked.

Grace had to stop herself from saying, *Thanks to you it didn't.*

"Everything happens in *Gott's* timing, Marlene. That's why you haven't had a *boppli* yet - because *Gott* is waiting for His perfect timing."

Marlene's jaw dropped in shock at what her mother-in-law had said. She threw the tea towel down on the sink and marched straight out of the room.

Seeing how upset Marlene was, Grace immediately felt sorry for her. "*Mamm,* that was a little harsh."

Her mother shrugged. "How would I know that she'd be upset by hearing about *Gott's* timing?"

"She's been married for nearly four years, and there's no *boppli*. It's only natural to be upset about that."

Marlene and Matthew had been married shortly after Jeremy and Grace. The last thing Jeremy had wanted was a baby, so they had been taking precautions, whereas that wasn't traditionally the way of the Amish.

Grace's mother shrugged her shoulders once again. "*Gott* waits for the timing of things to be right. Surely that should have been a comfort to her. She needs patience."

"Sometimes saying things like that don't help a person feel better. You never had any trouble having *bopplis*, so how could you understand someone who has?"

"Jebediah was born one year after your *vadder* and I got married. Then I had a new *boppli* almost every year or two after that. I suppose I shouldn't have said it, but sometimes Marlene just can't see any other side of things than her own." Her mother sighed. "I'll go and see if she's all right. And while I'm doing that, you make something delicious for our dessert tonight."

CHAPTER 5

But love ye your enemies, and do good, and lend, hoping for nothing again; and your reward shall be great, and ye shall be the children of the Highest: for he is kind unto the unthankful and to the evil.
Luke 6:35

WITH HER FAMILY and Adam at the dinner table, it felt like old times. Dinner was cabbage casserole, shepherd's pie, corn on the cob, and vegetables.

Grace had to force herself to eat because her stomach was squirmy. She noticed that Adam kept looking at her, and when she caught his eye, he smiled. He still gave her butterflies inside even after so many years had passed. Could things between them be restored and become what they should've been before Marlene had interfered?

Grace looked up at Marlene when her father said, "You're very quiet tonight, Marlene."

Marlene puffed out her full cheeks. "I'm feeling unwell, so if everyone will excuse me, I'll go to my room." Without waiting for any response, Marlene pushed out her chair, stood up, and then walked out of the room.

Matthew looked a little disturbed, excused himself, and then followed her.

"Did I say something wrong?" Grace's father whispered.

Then they heard Marlene's raised voice coming from the bedroom upstairs. To cover up, Grace's mother began talking about the quilting circle that Mrs. Schwartz ran and how she thought Grace should join. "Grace has made a lovely dessert."

Grace giggled. "I've made dessert, but I can't say that it'll be lovely. I made shoofly pies and cheesecake, and I haven't made them for years."

After dessert, Grace and Adam were told to sit out on the porch and wait for hot chocolate.

When they were both seated Grace rubbed her arms. "It's a bit chilly to sit out here."

"I think they got the idea we wanted to be alone. I hope me being here isn't upsetting Marlene."

"Nee, it wouldn't be. Why would you think that?"

"I was a little harsh on her this afternoon. With all

the trouble she caused between us she must feel pretty bad now."

"I don't know if she does. Maybe. I do know that right now she's upset about things that have nothing to do with you or me." It was a strange idea of her mother's to sit them out on the cold porch. The one advantage was the chill in the air was taking her mind off her unsettled tummy. "Do you still come here for dinner as often as you used to?"

He shook his head. "Every now and again I do, but not as often as when you were here. Grace, I want to spend the day with you tomorrow if you aren't doing anything. That is if you'd like to."

"Really?"

"*Jah*, really. I want to get to know you again. I want to hear what life has been like for you. I know you must've changed from the girl I once knew. You're older now, so you must have changed in some ways."

"I'm not so different. I think I'm just the same, maybe wiser, that's all. I appreciate what's important in life now. Also, I'm not impulsive like I used to be." She wanted him to know that she regretted her rash decision to run away with Jeremy.

"Can I come and collect you at nine in the morning?"

Grace could barely keep the smile off her face. "Nine will be good. Adam, I want you to know that I regret that I didn't stick around when things erupted between us years ago. I was so hurt that you chose to believe Marlene over me. I want you to know that…"

"Shh. You don't have to tell me anything right now. We have to leave something to talk about tomorrow."

"I'll look forward to it."

"Me too."

They were interrupted by Grace's mother bringing them out two mugs of hot chocolate.

"*Denke,* Mrs. Byler."

"*Jah, denke, Mamm.*"

"You're most welcome," she said before she disappeared inside.

For the second time in her life, Grace felt things were finally turning out right. The first time she'd felt like that was when she'd married Jeremy, but that had been a total disaster. She knew no relationship with Adam would ever be like that. Adam was reliable and trustworthy, and she knew he wasn't putting on a good show like Jeremy had before they'd married.

He took a sip from his steaming mug, and then he looked across at her and smiled. "I'll look forward to tomorrow."

CHAPTER 6

A merry heart doeth good like a medicine: but a broken spirit
drieth the bones.
Proverbs 17:22

THE NEXT MORNING, Grace was helping her mother with the breakfast when Marlene and Matthew came downstairs. Grace's father had already left for work early, as he normally did. Matthew worked for a building company and often didn't leave until eight in the morning.

"Did you hear the good news, Matthew?" his mother asked him.

"What good news is that?"

"Grace and Adam are spending the day together."

Grace pulled a face at her mother's remark.

"I suppose that's good news if that makes Grace happy. He's a *gut* man."

Marlene remained silent and squeezed past Grace and her mother to pour herself and her husband a cup of coffee. Then she sat down next to Matthew at the table.

"Would you like me to make you and Matthew some breakfast, Marlene?" Grace asked.

"I think I can look after my own husband well enough without your help, Grace."

Grace remained silent as she sat down at the table and began sipping on a cup of hot peppermint tea.

Matthew said, "If you two are going to be living under the same roof, you should try to get along with each other. I've talked to each of you and you've both said that you'd try, but neither of you seem to be putting any effort in."

Marlene jutted out her bottom jaw. "What did I say? She was making out I don't look after you well enough, and I do."

Grace remained silent, knowing that anything she said would be taken the wrong way. Not knowing where to look, she stared into her tea. Even though Grace's mother was in the kitchen as well, she didn't comment and busied herself at the kitchen sink.

Matthew shook his head. *"Nee,* Marlene, you're wrong. I can't agree with you because you're speaking nonsense. Grace was simply being nice by offering to cook breakfast for us, and you're twisting what she said to have a negative meaning."

"Why are you on her side?"

Matthew's mouth fell open at the way Marlene had raised her voice at him. "There are no sides to this. I'm on neither side; I'm simply stating what is reasonable to expect, and that is that the two of you should be getting along."

Marlene jumped to her feet. "Well, it seems I can't do anything to make you happy. Everything I try just isn't good enough for you, is it?"

"Sit down, Marlene! You're making a scene," he said.

"Making a scene? How's this for making a scene?" Marlene picked up her cup of coffee and threw it against the wall. Coffee went everywhere, and the broken pieces of crockery fell to the ground. Marlene wasn't finished there. She also picked up Matthew's half-drunk cup of coffee and threw it against the same wall. Then she ran out of the house.

Grace was not going to look into her brother's face. Her mother hurried to pick up the broken pieces of china while her brother sat staring after his wife.

"I didn't realize that would upset her so badly," he said.

"New marriages take a while. You both have to adjust to each other's ways."

"We've been married nearly four years, *Mamm*. It's hardly a new marriage."

"I think she was upset when you spoke against her

in front of everyone," Grace said. "Every wife just wants the support of her husband."

"That makes no sense. She was wrong, and I'm not going to pretend otherwise," Matthew said.

"From her point of view, being right or wrong has nothing to do with it. Aren't you going to go after her?" Grace asked.

He shook his head. "Not this time. I've grown tired of constantly trying to make her happy. It seems whatever I do or say is never good enough."

Grace wondered how often this type of thing happened. Grace knew if she had been upset like Marlene had been just now, she would've wanted her husband to run after her and make sure she was okay."

Grace stood up and looked out the kitchen window to see where Marlene was. She was far away in the fields and running; just a speck in the distance heading toward Adam's house. She turned back to Matthew. "I really think you should go after her."

"You don't know what's gone on between us, Grace. I've tried hard, but it's exhausting sometimes."

"It doesn't matter. She'd want you to comfort her. She just needs love and understanding."

He leaned over and whispered to Grace in a voice that their mother would not be able to hear, "And that's exactly why I'm not going to follow her this time."

Grace felt sorry for Marlene. She knew what it was like to want kindness from your husband, and get nothing but coldness. "Do you mind if I talk to her?"

"You can do that if you think it will help. Jump on one of the horses," Matthew said. "Take Charlie. He's the only one that doesn't mind being ridden."

Grace put her coat on and took the shawl that Marlene had left behind. She grabbed a bridle from the barn and placed it on Charlie, walked him near the fence and climbed on his bare back. She'd been a good rider years ago, but she never remembered her dress riding up as it was now.

She kept as far away from the roads as she could and cantered the horse bareback. When she drew close to Adam's house, she slid off Charlie. She didn't want Adam to see her with her dress up around the tops of her legs.

She wanted to be on her best behavior around Adam because of his high standards. As she led Charlie behind her, she caught sight of Marlene, who was climbing into a buggy parked outside Adam's front door. Grace stood and watched Marlene whip the ends of the reins against the horse's rump. The horse set off at an incredible speed.

CHAPTER 7

Beloved, I wish above all things that thou mayest prosper
and be in health, even as thy soul prospereth.
3 John 1:2

"What is she doing?" Grace asked out aloud as she watched Marlene steal Adam's buggy. Grace squinted to see which way Marlene would turn once she reached the end of the driveway. Right would mean she might head home, and left would mean she was heading elsewhere.

"She's not going home!" Grace knew she had a quick decision to make. She could involve Adam to have him go after her or turn back and tell Matthew what she'd seen. Since Matthew was already upset with Marlene, and she'd stolen Adam's buggy, Grace took the only course of action that seemed reasonable. She took hold of the horse's mane in one hand and leaped onto his back. Riding as fast as she comfortably could, she headed in the direction that Adam's buggy had taken.

Grace hoped that Marlene would slow the buggy down. If she'd had enough time to saddle Charlie, she could've caught up with the buggy in no time at all, but as it was, she'd have to hope that the buggy slowed.

She kept her eyes focused on the buggy heading away from her when she saw the buggy suddenly tip over.

"Marlene!" she screamed. When she got close, she jumped off Charlie and flung his reins around a tree branch, racing to see if Marlene was injured. The horse was on his side and trying to get up.

"Marlene!" she screamed once again.

"I'm okay," Marlene said as she appeared climbing over the side of the buggy.

Grace looked at the horse and hoped he didn't have a broken leg. She undid the straps that kept the horse trapped on the ground and he got to his feet. The horse appeared to be all right. She held on to his cheek-strap.

Marlene asked, "Where's Matthew?"

"Back at the *haus.*"

Marlene burst into tears. "Grace, don't tell Matthew that I did this. He doesn't love me anymore, and he'd be so disappointed in me. No one likes me; no one in your *familye* likes me. Your *mudder* keeps making cold remarks to me, and your *vadder* ignores me unless he's asking me if I'm all right. *Nee!* I'm not all right."

Grace noticed Adam running up the road toward them.

Marlene, still in tears, said, "Grace, please don't tell."

"What happened?" Adam looked them both up and down and then went straight to his horse. He crouched down and ran a hand down each of his legs. He stood up and looked directly at Grace, and repeated, "What happened?"

Grace took a deep breath. "I'd heard your horse was fast and I wanted to see how fast he could go. I'm sorry, I tipped the buggy over."

He looked at Marlene and then looked at the Byler's horse, Charlie. "How did you come to be here with Charlie, Marlene?"

"I was out riding Charlie when I came across Grace. I'm just glad she's okay. She could've gotten badly hurt. Do you think there's something wrong with your buggy to tip over suddenly like that with no warning?"

"*Nee*, there was nothing wrong with my buggy, but there is now." He pointed to the broken lights and twisted triangular reflector. "I'll have to get those repaired, and it looks like the suspension's damaged too."

"Are you sure it wasn't like that before?" Marlene asked.

"*Nee*, Marlene. I was cleaning the buggy this morning ready to take it out for the day. I would've noticed." Adam looked at Marlene and lifted an eyebrow. "I've never known you to ride, Marlene. Are you sure things didn't happen the other way around?"

"I do, I like horse-back riding. I ride quite often."

"Looks like my horse is all right, so that's something." Adam put his hands on his hips and stared down at his buggy.

"I better get home now to cook my husband's breakfast. He's waiting for me to come back from my ride." Marlene walked over and plucked Charlie's reins from the tree. She led the horse behind her as she walked away.

Grace didn't like lying, especially when she was making a commitment to God and being baptized in the not-too-distant future. Perhaps *Gott* would forgive her and overlook her lie if she was doing it to help her brother and sister-in-law's marriage.

"I'm sorry, Adam, I'm truly sorry. I don't know what came over me. I'll pay for the repairs of the buggy."

He shook his head. "*Nee*, you won't. That's not necessary. I'll take him home." He took hold of his horse's cheek strap and she took her hand away.

"Are you going to leave the buggy here?"

"I'll get Matthew or your *vadder* to give me a hand with that this afternoon. Looks like we'll have to delay that day out of ours. I'm sorry, Grace."

Grace could see he was bitterly disappointed in her. She knew he had more than one horse and more than one buggy. They still could've had their day out, but she was no longer in the mood and she couldn't blame him for not being in the mood either.

They walked alongside one another in silence until they reached Adam's long driveway.

"Well, I guess I'll spend the day helping *mamm* with chores."

Adam nodded. "Goodbye, Grace."

"Goodbye, Adam." They walked their separate ways.

Once again, Marlene had ruined everything. *What would Adam think of me, a grown woman, taking his buggy without asking? He must think I've lost my mind. I know Adam's looking for a sensible woman and now he thinks I'm anything but the kind of woman he's looking for.*

Just as she was about to turn into her driveway, Matthew was coming towards her in his buggy. He stopped when he drew level. "Thanks for going after her, Grace. I know I should've but sometimes I just get tired of her antics."

"Perhaps she would calm down if you made an extra effort to show her how much you love her. I'm not saying you don't do those things, but I know from being married that sometimes I just wanted to know he cared, and that's all I wanted. That would've been enough."

"You look so sad sometimes, Grace. One day you might tell me what's made you so unhappy. I'm guessing things between you and Jeremy were worse than you've let on."

Grace looked down at the dirt and small pebbles at her feet.

"I'll keep in mind what you said." Matthew clicked his horse onward and Grace continued home.

When Grace walked into the house, her mother said, "You better get ready for your day out with Adam. You can't wear that. Go and clean yourself up - he'll be here any minute."

"Something came up and Adam can't make it today, *Mamm.*" *Or any other day.*

"What came up so suddenly? We only saw him just last night."

"Adam and I just need to give things a little more time."

When her mother opened her mouth to say something, Grace put up her hands. "It has to be my decision and mine alone, *Mamm.* I'm not ready to think about another man. Jeremy has just died." Her eyes filled with tears and she ran upstairs to her bedroom. Part of her was crying for Jeremy and part of her was crying for Adam. Her second chance with Adam had been ruined, and ruined by the same person. But this time she had been a contributor. She could have told Adam the truth. After all, Marlene would never have taken the blame for her if their positions had been reversed.

Her mother knocked on her door and walked into her room without waiting for an answer. "You're right. It's just that I've always thought you and Adam would make a lovely couple. I didn't know Jeremy; you never brought him around. I'm sorry I've been insensitive to both you and Marlene. It's hard to remember how young women think. I'll try harder. I won't mention Adam again to you and I won't mention *kinner* to Marlene."

Grace sat up and hugged her mother. *"Denke.* That'll be a good start."

"But if you married Adam, you'd be living right next door." When Grace opened her mouth in shock at her mother, she said, "That's all I was going to say."

"Some things just aren't meant to happen." She looked down at her clothes and saw that they were smeared with dirt. "I'll change out of these grubby clothes and then I'll come down and help you with chores."

Her mother leaned down and kissed her on her forehead, and before she walked out of the room she said, "I'm so glad you're home."

When Grace was in the middle of changing her clothes, there was a quiet knock on her door. She opened her door a crack to see Marlene.

"Can I come in?"

Grace opened her door enough to let Marlene through. She sat down on Grace's bed. *"Denke* for what you did just now, Grace. It shows me that you truly want to be my friend. We were good friends once."

Grace had just changed her dress, now she was unfolding her apron. "I think I lost your shawl in the fields somewhere. I had it when I left and when I got home I didn't have it. I'll go out later to find it."

"It'll be there somewhere. I hope I haven't ruined things between you and Adam."

"Here, tie my apron." Grace turned around for Marlene to fix her apron. "It doesn't matter. Some things just aren't meant to be." Disappointment was something Grace was familiar with, and had learned to live with. Why should things be any different now?

"I know what you mean, like Matthew and I being happy and having a *boppli.*"

"No one tells you before you're married, but marriage is hard. That's what I found out. And having a baby, that's something I know nothing about."

"I tried to speak with your *mudder* about women's things, but she just doesn't understand. She had no problems having *kinner;* she doesn't know how hard it's been for me to see women who get married and right away have a *boppli* a year later – just like that. Betsy Yoder got married after me, and she's already got two *kinner* with another on the way."

Grace felt closer to Marlene now that she was opening up to her. She would have felt even more sorry for her if she hadn't just ruined things for her for a second time.

"Let's forget our troubles and go down to help *Mamm.*"

Marlene nodded.

For the next few hours, Grace tried to forget that

Adam now had the idea reinforced in his head that she was impulsive, not to mention careless with others' possessions. She'd have to go and make amends, and force him to accept payment for damages to his buggy. Grace was thankful his horse was unharmed.

CHAPTER 8

Confess your faults one to another, and pray one for another,
that ye may be healed.
The effectual fervent prayer of a righteous man availeth
much.
James 5:16

W<small>HEN</small> G<small>RACE</small>'<small>S</small> father came home for the midday meal, he mentioned that he'd come across Adam's tipped over buggy and had helped him get it home.

"Why did you do a silly thing like that, Grace? You've disgraced our *familye.*"

"I'm not certain, but I am going to his place this afternoon and make arrangements to pay for the damages."

"And you should, too. Looks like it'll be costly."

When Grace looked at Marlene on hearing that news, Marlene looked away from her, and kept quiet.

Grace had no money and had no idea how to come up with some to pay for the buggy repairs. All her savings had gone on Jeremy's funeral and paying out the remainder of the lease on their apartment. She had returned to the community from her life in the *Englisch* world without a dime. "I don't have any money though, *Dat.* I'm going to get a job soon; perhaps he won't mind waiting for the money."

"You'll have to work for him, then. Work around his *haus.* Make meals, clean, whatever you have to do. I don't want to be in debt to my neighbors. Have you finished eating?"

Grace nodded.

"Go and see him now. Marlene can help your *mudder* clean up here."

Marlene turned around, and said, *"Jah,* you go now, Grace. I'll help *Mamm* here."

Grace fixed a smile on her face. "That's nice of you, Marlene. I'll go and see him now." Grace walked out of the house and immediately a wave of nausea hit her. She ran to the garden in just enough time to be sick amongst the bushes. It would take a while for her to adjust to the different food she was eating. She rinsed her mouth out with cold water from the outside tap, splashed some on her face, and then continued to Adam's house. Before she got there, she found Marlene's black shawl. She picked it up and gave it a good shake before she put it around her shoulders.

When she reached Adam's house, she heard hammering coming from the barn. She poked her head in. "Hello?"

"I'm over here."

She walked in further, and saw him at the back of the barn, leaning over, working on the buggy. "Is there much damage?"

He stood up. "Quite a bit."

"I'm sorry."

"It's too late now to be sorry," he said, staring at the buggy.

"I'll pay for the damage."

He looked at her and pushed his hat back on his head. "There's no need to do that."

"I must. I must pay for the damage I caused."

He kept his eyes fixed on her while he lowered his head. "And you have the money?"

"I don't right now, but *Dat* suggested I should work for you to pay for it. Unless you'd rather wait for the money? I'm getting a job soon."

Adam laughed. "And what kind of work would you do for me?"

"Cook, clean, any kind of work around the place."

Adam licked his lips. "My *haus* is never as clean as I'd like it to be. It's hard to do everything on my own. I might just take you up on your offer."

"Great. That'll make me feel a lot better." Another

wave of nausea came over her. She put one hand to her stomach and covered her mouth with her other hand.

Adam took a step toward her. "What's wrong?"

She shook her head and ran out of the barn. Just as she got outside, she heaved up, and then heaved again.

He hurried over. "I'll get some water."

She was too sick to respond, and then she was sick again. After the third lot, she felt a little better. She wiped her mouth and stood up straight to see Adam heading back toward her with a glass of water and a concerned look on his face.

"Denke." She took the water from him and looked down at the ground where she'd just been sick. "This isn't a good start to helping you keep your place clean."

"Don't worry about that. I'll cover it with some sawdust now, and fix it later on. Come over and sit down on the porch. Rest for a while." When she sat down, he sat next to her. "Is there something wrong with you, Grace?"

"I think I'm eating too much since I got here, or maybe it's the different food. I didn't eat very much before I came back here. Now with all this food around, I'm eating a lot more. It takes the body a few weeks to adjust when you start eating totally different food."

Adam said, "Could you be pregnant?"

CHAPTER 9

Fear thou not; for I am with thee: be not dismayed; for I am thy God: I will strengthen thee; yea, I will help thee; yea, I will uphold thee with the right hand of my righteousness.
Isaiah 41:10

GRACE FROZE when Adam asked her if she could be pregnant. Her eyes opened wide, and her mouth fell open. She was embarrassed that he asked her that personal question so openly. "I don't think I could be."

"Is there a possibility? These things do happen, Grace. My aunt's a midwife and I've heard all kinds of stories."

"Nee. I couldn't possibly be. It's impossible."

"When did you say your husband died? Wasn't it only eight weeks ago?"

"Ten weeks now, but we weren't trying to get pregnant. In fact, we were trying not to." Grace knew that concept would be hard for Adam to grasp because none of the Amish used contraceptive interventions unless there were health reasons involved. A child was a blessing from God. It was then that it dawned on Grace that the physical symptoms she'd had might not have been due to stress or diet. "I suppose it *is* a possibility."

"You want me to arrange for Aunt Sarah to come and see you?"

"I couldn't. Then everybody would know."

He frowned.

"What I mean is everybody at my *haus* will know and I don't want to let them know that I might be pregnant."

"I could have Aunt Sarah come here and see you."

"Or I could just go and buy a test. I can just get one from a pharmacy, and then I'll know either way in minutes." Grace chewed on her lip, wishing she had a female friend she could have this conversation with.

"I'll drive you there right now."

Grace covered her face in her hands; this couldn't be happening. "I'm scared to find out."

"You being scared won't change the outcome. Either you are, or you aren't."

"I'll have to go back to the *haus* and get some money. You don't mind driving me?"

He stood up and offered her his hand. "Come on, I'll

even pay for it. I do have one buggy that you haven't broken."

Grace smiled and gave him her hand. He lifted her to her feet. Then there was an awkward moment when she didn't know if she should let go of his hand. They released each other's hand at the same time while they walked to the barn. Grace leaned on the fence watching Adam hitch the buggy.

"Don't look so worried," Adam said when they climbed into the buggy.

"I am worried. This could change my whole life." Grace nibbled at her fingernails.

"I'm a firm believer that the things that happen to us in this life are always for the best even if they appear that they're the worst thing that could possibly happen to you. A *boppli* is always a blessing from *Gott* even in your situation."

Grace nodded. As soon as he said those words, 'your situation' Grace knew that he'd had no thoughts of marriage to her. He thought of her as merely a friend who might be about to become a mother. Grace blew out a deep breath. She couldn't blame him. Besides, didn't she deserve someone who would believe her over Marlene? Surely the perfect man for her would never have believed Marlene's lies in the first place.

She felt Adam staring at her, so she looked at him, and he smiled at her. Grace smiled back, desperately wanting to tell him that it had been Marlene who'd wrecked his buggy, but she would continue to take the blame until Marlene confessed. Grace felt sorry for Marlene being so unsure of herself and her marriage. In a way, Marlene's anxiousness to please Matthew reminded Grace of the way she had wanted more than anything to please Jeremy.

When they pulled up in town, Adam said, "I'll wait here."

She stared at Adam as he handed her some money. *"Denke,* for doing this Adam. You're a *gut* friend."

"I'm sure you'd do the same for me. Not that you'd ever have to."

Grace gave a little laugh.

"Go on. Go now."

She was too scared to get out of the buggy and hesitated.

"Go!" he said, a little more sternly.

"I'm going." She got out of the buggy and entered the pharmacy, wondering what Jeremy would think of her life now. He would hate the fact that she'd returned to the community, and he'd hate the fact that she was friends with Adam. As she walked through the pharmacy she was grateful that there were few customers in the store. After she found what she was looking for, she rushed to the checkout.

After she paid, they wrapped it in a paper bag and she took it back to the buggy where Adam had been waiting patiently.

"Now what happens?" Adam asked.

"We go back to your place, and I'll do the test there. I can't go back to my place."

"Okay."

As Adam drove back home, Grace stared at the paper package in her hands in silence. This was the first time she'd had need of such a test. In a few minutes, her life might change forever.

"Here we are," Adam said, when he pulled up back at his house. "I'm guessing you'll need to use the bathroom?"

She nodded.

"Upstairs on the left."

"I remember."

"I'll wait on the porch."

Ten minutes later, Grace was sitting on the bathroom floor, not game to look at the test-stick. It was a four-minute processing time, and it was already past the five-minute mark. Despite her nerves, she knew that if the test was negative she would be disappointed.

She prayed a silent prayer. A single line meant she was not pregnant, and a two-line plus sign meant that she was. She turned it over and saw a plus sign. It was a miracle.

After she'd stared at the stick for a while, she threw it in the trash and went outside to tell Adam her news. She'd hoped that what she and Adam had once might be rekindled, but all hopes of that had been dashed with the recent buggy incident thanks to Marlene. Carrying another man's baby would most likely drive another wedge between them and push Adam even further away. But now her baby was her main priority and her feelings for Adam had to be pushed to one side.

He jumped to his feet when she came out his front door toward him. He raised his eyebrows, wanting to know the outcome.

"The test was positive," she said collapsing into the porch chair next to the one he'd been sitting in.

"That's wonderful news."

"Jah, it is." She stared into his eyes and then looked out across his land into the distance.

"You should go and tell your family straightaway." Adam added, "And you should also go and see my aunty."

"Maybe I should see her first just in case the test was wrong. I don't want to get everybody's hopes up and then find out that there is no baby."

Adam nodded. "Do you want me to take you to see her tomorrow? I could call her right now and tell her that we're coming."

"Would you do that?"

He nodded. "I will."

"Denke." Grace's eyes suddenly filled with tears; she was having a baby. She had always wanted one, but Jeremy never had, and she'd only found out that information after they'd married. She'd assumed that everybody wanted babies. He had wanted to wait until they were in their thirties before they were tied down with what he called 'ankle-biters.'

"Grace, what's wrong?" He crouched down next to her.

"I think I'm happy." She wiped her tears away. "These are happy tears."

"It does explain why you've been sick."

"You're an expert, are you?" she asked with a laugh.

Adam chuckled. "I told you, my aunty told me some stories, and now I guess I am an expert."

Again she was gripped by the urge to tell him that it had been Marlene who had driven his buggy like a mad woman, but she couldn't.

"What time tomorrow should we go and see your Aunt Sarah?"

"You stay right there. I'm going to go into the barn right now to call her." Adam stood up and headed towards the barn.

Grace called after him. "Tell her she can't tell anyone I'm coming to see her."

Without turning around, he waved a hand in the air, and said, "I know. I know."

When he returned a few minutes later, Grace said, "Can she see us? I mean me?"

"Midday tomorrow. Will you be able to get away?"

"I will if I tell them I'm going out somewhere with you."

Adam chuckled. "Like that, is it?"

"A little bit. I hope I'm not keeping you from your work?"

"I took the day off, and I'll take some time off tomorrow as well."

"You don't work the farm anymore?"

"I leased it. It was too big for me to handle by myself. My cousin, Rupert, and I run a mill on his property."

"I didn't know that."

"I thought Matthew might've mentioned it. He worked for us for a little while."

"I didn't know that," Grace repeated. "I've been gone for so long and so many things have changed."

"Things don't change that quickly around here," he said with a smile.

"That makes it seem as though I've being gone longer. Well, I better leave you alone. I'm sure you've got things to do."

Adam opened his mouth to speak, but then hesitated. Grace felt that he wanted her to stay around but his common sense had prevailed. She stood up and so did he.

"I'll collect you at fifteen minutes before eleven tomorrow."

"I appreciate all you've done." She walked a few steps away from him, and then turned around. "Goodbye."

"Wait!"

She hoped he would say that he wanted her to stay a little longer. Perhaps he would invite her to stay for something to eat?

"I'll drive you home."

"Nee, it's hardly any distance at all. The walk will do me good."

Rather than going directly home, she walked farther into the fields that separated the two properties. She took some time to sit by the stream so she could sort things out in her mind. It seemed as though Jeremy was somehow still in control. Even in death he was affecting her life. She couldn't let this baby be a constant reminder of the dreadful marriage she'd had.

This baby is mine and now, mine alone. She knew now in her heart, that she was having a baby. The tests were highly accurate. Grace placed both hands over her baby and looked down. She would not let Jeremy ruin this time for her.

She looked over at the water gently rippling, wondering what God had in store for her and her baby.

The one thing she hoped for was that God would give her a place to stay where she felt she belonged. She no longer felt comfortable living with her parents. It was hard to live there with Marlene constantly getting under her skin. Now that she was having a baby, she wondered if her parents would still chastise her and tell her what to do as they had always done.

Adam's carving in the tree caught her eye as she stood to walk back home. Now, rather than a symbol of their love, it was a symbol of another wrong turn in her life. Once again she berated herself for reacting so hastily to Adam believing those lies. She was living a life she'd never thought she'd have. Her life was supposed to go just as her brothers' lives had gone. They had met their loved ones, married, and had babies. Why had that simple formula been so hard for her to follow?

CHAPTER 10

And above all things have fervent charity among yourselves:
for charity shall cover the multitude of sins.
1 Peter 4:8

WHEN SHE COULD STAY AWAY NO LONGER, she wandered home right when her mother and Marlene were cleaning up after the midday meal.

"You were gone for a long time," her mother said to her in a stern tone.

"Jah, it took a long time to apologize to Adam."

"What did he say?" her mother asked.

"In payment for the damages to his buggy, I have to clean his *haus* and do chores."

Her mother nodded. "You can go outside with the broom. Marlene, you go with her. There are some cobwebs around the side of the house and they look untidy."

"Follow me," Marlene said. "I know where everything is kept. I've been reorganizing things."

Once they were outside, Marlene said, "*Denke* so much for taking the blame for that, Grace. Now everyone's so mad at you they're being nice to me. It's a nice change."

Grace rolled her eyes. "That's hardly fair, Marlene. You should tell them that it was you. It's not fair that I get the blame."

Marlene pouted. "I'll tell everybody I did it, but can I just wait a little longer? I feel like such an outsider around your *familye*, and this is the only time I've felt that I belong. And even Matthew's been nice to me. He hasn't been nice to me for a long time." Marlene leaned in and whispered, "We're trying to have a baby, and that's not going to happen if Matthew's not happy with me, if you know what I mean."

Grace put her hands over her ears. "Ohhh, Marlene, I don't need to hear things like that."

Marlene giggled. "You've been married – you should know about these things."

Grace shook her head. "I don't want to hear about them, things like that."

"Here!" Marlene said as she handed Grace the broom. "Get those cobwebs down."

"Gladly, if you'll change the topic of conversation."

Marlene giggled again. "When do you have to start doing jobs for Adam?"

"He's picking me up tomorrow just before eleven."

"Can't you walk? It only takes five or ten minutes to walk to his house."

"I think he said that he's coming back from somewhere and then he's collecting me on his way home."

"I see. Well, I've done you a favor then, haven't I? You like Adam, and now you'll be seeing a lot more of him. You should thank me."

"What makes you think I like him?"

"I can tell you still like him, and he still likes you. He kept looking at you all the way through dinner last night."

Grace stopped sweeping the cobwebs off the house. She leaned on the broom. "Do you really think so?"

"*Jah.* I do. I know about love."

"Then you will know how important it is that you tell everyone that it was you and not me who damaged his buggy."

"I don't see what you mean. Isn't it better that everyone thinks it was you? No one in your *familye* will be mad at you for long and Adam adores you, so he'll forgive you. Matthew would be mad at me, and I can tell that your parents don't think highly of me. They're nice enough to my face, but they don't treat me as nicely as they treat their other *dochder*-in-laws."

"That's not true at all. They treat everyone the same. I do know that Adam wouldn't be interested in a woman who stole his good horse and buggy to gallop it away and then crash it. I'm already so far away from what he wants in a *fraa*."

"*Nee*, that's not true."

"It is. I left the community for years, married someone else, and now…" her voice trailed away.

"And now what?"

Grace shook her head and turned away from Marlene. "It's nothing."

"I can tell it's something. What were you about to say?"

Grace turned back and faced the sidewall of the house. She'd already gotten rid of the cobwebs so she started sweeping away some imaginary ones.

Marlene grabbed Grace's arm. "Grace, tell me what's going on." She swung Grace around to face her.

"You're hurting me, Marlene."

"Tell me what's going on; I know that there's something. If you don't tell me, I'll tell your *mudder* and *vadder* you're hiding something from them. They don't like secrets being kept."

"I don't know if there's anything to tell, yet."

Marlene tipped her head to the side and screwed up her round face. "What are you talking about, Grace? You're not making any sense at all."

"If I tell you something, you must keep it a secret. And if it turns out to be true, I must be the one to tell my family first, and not you. Okay?"

Marlene nodded and her eyes grew wide.

"And if you do tell everyone before I tell them, I'll tell everyone that it was you who drove Adam's buggy off the road. Fair enough?"

"All right, just tell me."

Normally Grace would not have shared anything with Marlene, but maybe sharing something so personal could turn things around for their friendship. "I think I might be pregnant."

Marlene's jaw dropped open and she stared at Grace in disbelief without saying a word.

Grace went on to explain, "Of course, it'll be Jeremy's baby."

Marlene stared at her for a few more seconds before she grabbed the broom from Grace's hands, threw it into the garden, and stomped away from her without saying a word. When Grace picked up the broom, she heard a door slam from inside the house. It was then that Grace recalled that Marlene had been upset with Grace's mother recently for making a comment about her not having a baby.

I'm so stupid. I shouldn't have said anything. She's been trying to have one, and if I am having one that will make her feel even worse.

She knew she had to talk to Marlene. Grace propped the broom up, and headed inside to come face-to-face with her mother.

"I can't leave you two alone for five minutes. Why is she upset now?"

"I said something thoughtless. I'm going right

upstairs to apologize to her now."

Her mother gave a sharp nod of her head. "And so you should. And then you can both come down and help me with dinner."

"Yes, *Mamm*."

Grace climbed the stairs and made her way to Marlene's door. She raised her hand and knocked quietly.

A couple seconds later. Marlene opened the door a crack. *"Jah?"*

"Can we talk for a minute?"

Marlene opened the door wider, and then sat back down on the bed. Grace walked in and sat down on the bed next to her.

"I'm sorry, Marlene. I forgot for a moment that you are upset about not having a *boppli* yet."

Marlene swallowed hard and nodded.

Grace added, "I might not be."

"What makes you think that you are?"

"I did a test, but maybe it's not accurate. I suppose there's a chance it might not be."

"I think those things are pretty accurate these days, Grace."

Grace noticed more tears brimming in Marlene's eyes.

"I'm so selfish, Grace. I should be happy for you, but I'm just sad for myself." Marlene sniffed and sat straighter.

"I understand how it must feel." Grace tried to

comfort Marlene by rubbing her on her shoulder. She wanted to tell Marlene that she didn't get pregnant deliberately, but that might have just made Marlene feel worse. She searched her mind for something that would give her sister-in-law comfort.

"You will be pregnant. Everything always works out for you, Grace."

Grace's mouth dropped open. "It does not. It's just the opposite. I lost Adam, and then I married Jeremy, and that was a terrible mistake." Grace bit her lip. She was supposed to be comforting Marlene and not going over her woes again. "Everything will work out for you. You married my *bruder,* and he's a *wunderbaar* man.

"*Jah*, he is, but he's not happy with me."

"Of course he is. He loves you."

"Things aren't the same as when we first married."

"It's probably because you're living here; it can't be easy. Things will get much better when you get your own home."

"And when will that be? Matthew said it would be another two years."

Grace recalled that Matthew had said he was annoyed with Marlene for not getting a job to help them save money. "It'll be quicker if you get a job away from the home."

"I didn't get married to work outside the home. I help *Mamm* look after the *haus* and I look after Matthew."

"That's good, but that doesn't bring in any money.

I'm here now to help *Mamm,* so why not look for a job, even a part-time job? It'll help you get your own home faster. Doesn't that sound good?"

"You'll be living the life that I want to live, Grace. Can't you see that? You'll be home here with *Mamm* doing the cooking and you'll have a *boppli.* That's what I want; I don't want a job. That's not like the kind of life I wanted."

"It'll only be for a while. If you get a job, you might be in your own home in under a year and then you can have your *boppli* in your own home." Grace did her best to make it sound an exciting thing to do.

"What kind of job would I get? I don't know how to do anything. I don't have any particular skills."

"You can cook. Why don't you set up a roadside stall like many people in the community do? You can sell jams and preserves. *Mamm* used to do that a few years ago. That way, you'll have your own business and can work your own hours. I'm sure *Mamm* will let you use the kitchen for that."

Immediately, Marlene's face brightened. *"Jah.* I think that is something that I'd like to do. Would you help me?"

"Of course I'll help you. Let's go down now and ask *Mamm* if we can use her kitchen."

The two girls went down and discussed the idea of a roadside stall with Grace's mother who was excited by the idea. They set about planning what they would make.

CHAPTER 11

For God so loved the world, that he gave his only begotten
Son, that whosoever believeth in him should not perish,
but have everlasting life.
John 3:16

As she'd said, Marlene had kept her word and had not breathed a word of Grace's secret. Grace's mother was delighted to hear that she was going to spend a great deal of the day with Adam. Everyone except Marlene thought this was to be Grace's first day doing chores for Adam in payment for the buggy repairs. Grace had been sick that morning as soon as she woke up, but was certain that no one had heard.

Right on a quarter to eleven, Grace heard the clip-clopping of horse's hooves and knew it was Adam. It was an hour-long trip to his Aunt Sarah's house.

"Ready to go, then?" Adam asked when Grace approached his buggy.

As she climbed up next to him, she said, "My body is ready, but I don't think my head is ready to find anything out."

On the way, Grace was thankful that Adam kept talking about topics other than the reason she was going to his aunt's house. Even though the pregnancy test was supposed to be highly accurate, if the midwife said she was having a baby, then she'd know without a doubt that she was.

When they arrived, Adam walked ahead of her and knocked on the door. While he waited for the door to be answered, he turned around and smiled at Grace who was walking toward him. "Don't be nervous. I'll wait out here on the porch."

Grace smiled at him and nodded. It was easy for him to say not to be nervous.

Aunt Sarah came to the door. "Come in, Grace." She looked at Adam. "You coming in too?"

"I'll wait on the porch."

"You can fix yourself something while you wait. You know where the kitchen is." She left Adam outside and walked further into the house with Grace. "I heard you'd come back to the community, Grace. Everyone's so happy that you're back. I was very sorry to hear about your husband dying."

"*Denke.* It was a car accident."

Sarah nodded. "I heard about it. It must have come as a horrible shock."

"It was. And now I think I might be pregnant. I did a test from the pharmacy and it was positive, but I don't know if those things can be trusted or not."

"They're usually accurate unless the test came into contact with some kind of chemical."

The midwife had Grace lie down and did an initial examination by pressing on Grace's abdomen. Sarah laughed. "Well I don't think there's much doubt about it, Grace, you're a good five months along."

"No! I can't be."

"And why is that?"

"Five months! That's nearly half way through isn't it?" Grace sat up.

"*Jah,* more than halfway."

Grace touched her belly. "I'm not that big."

"Many women in their first pregnancies hardly show at all, and with you being so thin it's not unusual for you to be barely showing."

"I thought I'd put on weight because of the different food I've been eating. It's quite unbelievable. I didn't have any signs."

"Adam said you've been sick."

"I have been. Not every day, though."

"Morning sickness is not really just *morning* sickness – it's common to get it at other times of the day. It usually disappears as your pregnancy progresses, but not always."

"I can't believe this is happening. I can't believe it's real. This wasn't planned. We were taking precautions."

"The only precaution that is one hundred percent reliable is abstinence."

"Well, I know that now. She looked down at her belly. "You said I was halfway?"

Sarah nodded. "Come and see me again in one month's time. Or before that, if you have any questions."

"And would you be able to deliver my baby?"

"I'd be happy to. Do you want to have the birth at home or at a birthing center?"

"I'd prefer to have my baby at home. *Mamm* had all hers at home."

"It's statistically safer than having your baby in the hospital, but it's something you have to feel comfortable about. I'll send you for an ultrasound in a few more weeks, and if everything looks normal, there'll be no reason why you can't have your baby at home. As long as that's still what you want to do."

Grace stood up.

"You can have a think about it let me know later. I think Adam's waiting for you on the porch. I'd invite you both in and spend some time with you, but I've got an appointment in town."

"Sarah, what are the payment arrangements for you being the midwife?"

"We'll talk about that later. You can pay after the birth. And don't worry; it won't be a fortune. I don't do all that much work anymore. Not now that Norma Jeter has moved to the community. She's younger and seems to relate more to the younger women. Anyway, working less suits me just fine."

"Denke, Sarah. I'm pleased that you're going to be my midwife. I know you, and I don't know Norma." After Sarah said goodbye, Grace made her way out the door to find Adam still on the porch. He jumped to his feet as soon as she came out the door.

She smiled when she saw the interest on his face. She nodded.

He said, "Grace, that's *wunderbaar* news." He was so excited that he touched her gently on her arm, and then leaned over to kiss her softly on her cheek.

"Sarah said that I'm five months along."

"Five months? Then you've not got long to go."

"That's right, which means I can't really delay telling everyone much longer."

On the way home, Grace wanted to make sure that she made things right with Adam. "Adam, I want to pay off my debt to you."

He waved a hand in the air to dismiss what she said. "Don't be ridiculous."

"I'm not being ridiculous. I'll come and do chores for you every day and cook meals for you."

"Nee. I don't want you to do anything of the kind."

She bit the inside of her lip, and then said, "I was

the one who wrecked your buggy so I should be the one to pay for it." She didn't like having to say those words but that's what he thought had happened, and until Marlene confessed, Grace would have to do the right thing in Adam's eyes.

Adam glanced over at her. "We've always been good friends, Grace, you and I; a broken buggy is not going to change that."

"I insist on paying off my debt. Besides, my *vadder* told me I should, and I'm not going to go against what he said."

Adam shrugged. "If you insist. You don't have to look far inside the house to find things to do."

Grace giggled. "That bad, is it?"

"It is. In fact, it's worse." Adam glanced over at her and smiled. "You can make a start tomorrow if you like. I'll leave the door unlocked when I leave for work."

"Okay, that'll be good." Grace was pleased that Adam hadn't asked her how she felt about having a baby, because she was still trying to sort out her feelings. She was amazed and scared all at the same time, plus a little pleased.

"Your parents will be happy."

"They certainly will be. I think this makes their tenth *kinskind*."

"That many already?"

Grace nodded. "This little one will have plenty of children to play with."

When Adam pulled up the buggy in front of Grace's house, she asked, "Will you come in?"

He shook his head. "I have to go to work. I can't have too much time off."

Grace climbed down from the buggy. Before he drove off, she called out, "I'll be there tomorrow."

He waved a hand in the air to acknowledge that he'd heard what she'd said.

As soon as Grace stepped onto the porch, the door flung open and she was faced with Marlene. "Well?"

Grace didn't feel right telling Marlene before she told the rest of the family. She figured her mother and father should be the first to know, but it was hours until her father got home.

"I can't say anything right now."

Marlene's button-like nose screwed up. "What do you mean?"

"I'll say something when everybody's together tonight," Grace responded.

Marlene wouldn't move out of the doorway. "That means you are, otherwise you wouldn't have anything to tell everyone."

"Please, Marlene. Will you let me pass?"

"Not until you tell me whether you are, or you aren't."

"Don't you remember that conversation we had?" She'd told Marlene that if she found out she was expecting, she wouldn't let Marlene know first, and Marlene had agreed.

"About?"

Without saying anything further, Grace raced around to the back door feeling very pleased with herself, but before she got there, Marlene flung the door open and stood in the doorway. She smirked with her arms folded.

Grace also folded her arms. "Can't you give me some privacy and respect?"

Marlene's arms fell down by her side as her jaw dropped open. "What do you mean?"

"I said that I just don't want to talk about it right now until everybody's together."

Marlene put one hand on her hip. "So you are? And you don't want to tell me first?"

"Would you tell me first?"

Tears came to Marlene's eyes and then she turned and ran into the house.

Grace stepped inside feeling dreadful. She hadn't meant to upset Marlene, but she didn't want Marlene to know before her parents. Why couldn't she understand that?

As soon as Grace went into the kitchen, her mother said, "What have you done to upset Marlene now?"

"I didn't mean to upset her. Seems everything I do upsets someone."

"Go upstairs and make sure she's all right. Bring her back down so she can help put up all this jam."

Grace looked at the sea of empty bottles that covered their large kitchen table before she trudged up the stairs. The midwife knew, Adam knew, so was it so bad to let her sister-in-law in on the secret? Grace knocked quietly on Marlene's door. Marlene opened the door while wiping tears from her eyes.

"Can I come in?" Grace asked.

Marlene opened the door wider.

Both girls sat on the bed. Grace said, "I'm having a *boppli.*"

Marlene flung her arms around her. "Grace, I'm so happy for you." Tears streamed down Marlene's face. She wiped her face with the end of her apron. "Did you tell me before you told anyone else?"

Grace nodded. "Only Sarah, the midwife, knows, and Adam because he had to take me there."

"Adam drove you to Sarah's house?"

"Sarah is Adam's aunt."

"That's right, she is."

"I'm going to tell everyone at dinner tonight."

"Can I tell Matthew when he comes home?"

"*Nee.* It's my news to tell; you can't tell anybody."

"Are you excited, Grace?"

"I don't know what I am." She looked at Marlene's face and immediately added, "I'm sure I'll be excited when I get used to the idea." She didn't want to appear too excited, nor did she want Marlene to think she didn't appreciate the gift God had given her. "Now come downstairs with me, Marlene. Wipe those tears away because you're going to be an aunt in four months."

"Four months? That's so soon. How come you've only found out about it now?"

"Because I'm stupid. I missed all the signs, thinking they were due to stress, and different food, and things like that. Anyway, let's go."

Marlene and Grace walked downstairs arm-in-arm. Grace was pleased that she'd shared her news with Marlene. Maybe Marlene had felt shut out and all she needed was to feel like part of the family. Grace hoped so.

CHAPTER 12

There is therefore now no condemnation to them which are
in Christ Jesus, who walk not after the flesh,
but after the Spirit.
Romans 8:1

WHILE GRACE HELPED WITH DINNER, she found it hard to concentrate on what she was doing. All she could think about was how to break the news to her family. It would come as a complete surprise to them.

Later, when everyone sat down at the table to eat, she had second thoughts. Maybe over the dinner table wasn't the right place to tell them. After dinner might be better. Grace looked over at Marlene who gave her a nod telling her to go ahead and tell them. Perhaps if she didn't say something right now, Marlene would.

Grace cleared her throat. "I have some news to tell everybody." Everybody fastened their eyes on her waiting for her to continue. There was nothing else for it she closed her eyes for an instant, and said, "I'm having a baby."

Her mother dropped her fork onto her plate and her mouth fell open in shock. Her father smiled and so did Matthew.

Marlene leaped off her chair and hugged Grace as though this were the first time she'd heard the news. "Grace, that's wonderful news!"

"*Denke*, Marlene.

Her mother frowned. "And how far are you along?"

"Five months."

"Five months? And you're just telling us now?"

"I've only just found out."

Her mother's face broke into a smile. "I'm pleased, of course, I'm pleased. I'm just shocked."

Her mother, father, and Matthew took turns to hug her.

"We're going to have a *boppli*!" her mother said, her hands pressed together.

Matthew put his arm around Marlene, and Grace was pleased that he was being sensitive of Marlene's feelings, knowing how much she wanted a baby. He knew Marlene might have been a little upset by the news of her sister-in-law being pregnant before she was.

"You don't look any bigger," her mother said. "But that's probably because you're so thin anyway."

"I won't be like that for much longer."

Everyone laughed.

THE NEXT DAY, as Grace said she would, she made her way to Adam's house clutching a packed lunch and a thermos of coffee. The walk over the open fields always reminded her of her childhood. Having no siblings to play with, Adam had always joined her older brothers as they made up games to play after school.

Seeing his regular buggy horse gone from the paddock, she knew that Adam had already left for work. She made her way up his front steps, and then pushed his door open. Once she was inside, she saw that the place was tidy, but it was covered in a thin layer of dust. Grace got to work right away, starting her cleaning in the kitchen. It was a big home for one person. Grace was certain that Adam's parents had planned for a much larger family, but Adam had remained their only child. She had been too young at the time to know the details of why they couldn't have other children, and now it didn't seem appropriate to ask Adam.

After hours of cleaning downstairs, she started scrubbing the boards of the stairs. She decided that once she finished the stairs, it would be time to go home. She started at the top and by the time she was halfway down, the front door opened.

"You're still here?"

She looked across to see Adam. "I'm sorry. I thought I'd be gone by the time you got home."

He placed his hands on his hips and looked around. "The place looks so clean! *Denke,* Grace, you've done a fine job. I feel horribly guilty about you doing all this. It's not necessary."

"It is necessary."

"Finish up now and I'll make us a cup of coffee. Do you have time to join me for a cup out on the porch?"

"I do."

While Adam headed to the kitchen, Grace collected her bucket, scrubbing brush and rags so she could rinse them under the outside tap. Once she'd done that, she left them near the tap to dry and sat on the porch.

Minutes later, Adam returned with two mugs of coffee and handed one to her. "You didn't bring your own lunch, did you?"

"I did. I wasn't sure how long I'd be here."

He shook his head. "Now I feel even worse. I'm taking advantage of you when you should be taking things easy."

"I'm fine. I have to do something, and besides, it's nice and peaceful here."

"Did you tell your parents your news last night?"

"I did, and they're pleased."

"Of course. Did you think they wouldn't be?"

"It's just that Jeremy was an *Englischer* and I'd left the community to be with him."

"And now you're back and you going to get baptized pretty soon, so nothing else matters does it?"

"That's right I guess; nothing else matters."

"I came home early today because I hoped you would still be here so we could talk." He looked across at her.

"You did?"

He nodded.

"Do you have something on your mind?"

He looked out across the fields, then he glanced back at her. "I just like your company."

Grace knew him well enough to know he had something to say to her other than just liking her company. She wondered what it was that he wanted to say.

They stayed and talked on the porch for a while, and then Adam walked Grace home.

GRACE'S first Sunday meeting since she'd been home was being held at the Schwartzes' house. The Schwartzes had moved to the community after Grace had left. Grace was anxious to talk to the bishop and tell him she wanted to be baptized as soon as she could. She wanted her commitment to God made as early as possible. She caught sight of him and walked over. He agreed to move the baptism to four weeks away, but she'd have to have instructions two nights a week, rather than one, leading up to the baptism.

Grace entered the house and sat in the back row. All the furniture had been moved out of the main room and the men had moved the long wooden benches in. As usual, the men were on one side and the women on the other. She looked over at Adam who was a few rows in front of her and to the other side. There were only a few minutes to go before the service started. Grace was jolted from her daydreams when someone shoved her arm. She looked up to see Marlene.

"Shove over. I suppose I'll have to sit next to you since no one else is," Marlene said.

Grace's mother always sat in the front row next to her best friend, Nellie.

Grace moved along. "*Denke*, Marlene. It's nice to have someone to sit next to." Grace looked over at Adam again and saw Matthew was now sitting next to him.

The deacon stood and said a prayer. Grace said a silent prayer of thanks for her baby. Out of her marriage to Jeremy, something good had come. After hymns were sung, the bishop preached. He spoke on love, and putting others first. Grace felt that God was telling her to be nice to Marlene even though Marlene had wronged her.

When the service was over, Grace made sure she was one of the first out the door as she was overcome by nausea. She walked away from the house to stand by the buggy. Marlene had followed close behind.

"Grace, what's wrong?"

"Go back. It's nothing; I'm just feeling a little queasy."

"Will I get Sarah, the midwife? She's here today. I saw her."

Being too sick to answer, Grace could only move her head slightly to say no. Grace went behind the buggy and was sick in the Schwartzes' garden. After she was sick twice more, she felt better.

When Grace stood up straight she saw that Marlene had moved closer.

"I'll take you home. You can't stand out here in the cold like this – you'll catch your death. I'll have Matthew go home with *Mamm* and *Dat* and I'll take you home right now."

"*Denke.* I could do with some sleep. I'm so tired now."

"I'll go tell them what's happening."

Grace watched Marlene hurry back to the house. She looked among the crowd coming out of the house, but couldn't see Adam anywhere.

GRACE WAS thankful to be lying in her own bed. She heard footsteps in her room and opened her eyes slightly to see Marlene approaching with an extra quilt.

Without saying anything, Marlene covered her with it and then crept out.

She hoped Marlene would tell Adam what really happened with the buggy. Marlene was being friendly and caring toward her now, so perhaps she would. Otherwise Grace would have to keep cleaning Adam's house until the debt was paid.

Grace woke feeling much better. She heard a commotion downstairs and wondered what it was. She pulled on her prayer *kapp*, fixed her apron over her dress and made her way down the stairs. When she walked into the kitchen she saw Marlene rearranging the saucepan cupboard.

She looked up when Grace entered the room. "Wake you, did I?"

Grace yawned, and stretched her hands above her head. "*Nee.* I had a good sleep. *Denke* for bringing me home. *Mamm* and *Dat* not home yet?" Grace sat down at the table.

"*Nee*, they're out visiting."

"And Matthew?"

"He's over at Adam's house helping him with something."

"What's he helping him with?"

Marlene winced. "He's helping him with the buggy."

Grace knew that Marlene was feeling bad about things so Grace didn't say any more about it. Marlene would admit to it when she was ready.

Marlene sat down at the table next to Grace. *"Denke* for keeping our secret about me crashing the buggy."

Grace nodded. And had second thoughts about Marlene ever confessing her wrongdoing. "It put me in a really bad light with Adam."

"Jah. I know, but if I tell everybody I did it, then my husband will be upset with me. No one will be upset with you."

"But you're already married, and I thought Adam and I might've had a second chance. We liked each other once. That is, until you told him I was sneaking off to see an *Englischer."* Marlene had forced her to say more than she'd wanted.

Marlene remained silent and stared back at her with large green eyes.

Grace kept talking, hoping to get through to her. "This could be my last chance with Adam. Can you see how I feel, at all?"

"Don't put it like that, Grace. You're being so dramatic. I'll heat up some soup for you."

Grace knew it was no use; Marlene had no intention of ever telling anybody the truth of what had happened. And now Grace would remain a fool in Adam's eyes.

CHAPTER 13

If ye know these things,
happy are ye if ye do them.
John 13:17

THE NEXT MORNING, Grace left Marlene and her mother cooking jam while she wrapped herself in a blanket and set off for Adam's house to do more chores. All she wanted to do was go back to sleep.

When she reached Adam's front door, she was half hoping that he would have forgotten to keep the door unlocked so she would have an excuse to go home again. Unfortunately, that wasn't the case – he'd left the door open. She walked through the doorway and saw that he'd left the fire going for her. From the way the fire was raging, Grace could tell that Adam wasn't long gone.

She stood by the fire to warm herself while she wondered where to start. She decided to finish the stairs and then clean the windows before heading upstairs. On her last visit there when Adam had walked her home, she'd made him agree that she could keep working there until the debt was paid. He'd agreed on the condition that she only do two hours at a time.

When Grace was ready to go home, she swung the blanket back over her shoulders and stepped out onto the porch. She was a little disappointed that she wouldn't see him that day. On her way home, she remembered that she had to go to the bishop's house that night for the Bible study. Soon her new life of being a baptized member of her Amish community would begin.

MATTHEW DROVE her and stayed with her while she took the Bible study. There were four others doing the three-hour session.

It was ten o'clock before it ended.

As soon as they climbed into the buggy to go home, Matthew said, "Do you know how much it's going to cost to fix Adam's buggy?"

"Why are you only talking about this now? If you know, you should've told me before."

Matthew clicked his horse forward. "I didn't know whether I should tell you or not. I've been thinking it over this whole time while I was waiting for you."

"Well, how much?"

"Nine hundred dollars."

"That is a lot."

"I can't imagine how bad it must have been for Adam to see you racing up the street in the buggy. What got into you?"

Grace shrugged her shoulders. "I don't know. Might be the hormones. I must've gone a little crazy."

"More than a little," Matthew added. "Anyway, I'm glad you and Marlene are finally starting to get along."

"We are getting along better. She's been very kind to me."

"She was a little upset to hear that you're having a *boppli.* I mean, she was happy for you, but a little disappointed for us that we don't have one yet."

"*Jah.* I can imagine how she'd feel. It must be upsetting for her."

"I told her not to worry about it. If it happens it happens, and if it doesn't it doesn't. We've got more than enough nieces and nephews running around to look after."

"She needs to know that you don't blame her, that you'll love her just as much if she's never able to give you a child." What she had just said made him think. Grace knew that by the look on her brother's face. In true male fashion, he swallowed hard and remained silent.

Grace hadn't seen Adam for over a week when her mother said, "Now, Grace, I've made you a nice meal to take over to Adam."

"I thought you were cooking far too much," Grace said. "It's a bit late, isn't it? He might already have something arranged for dinner."

Her father put his paper on his lap, and said to his wife, "It's too cold for her to go out now. We're expecting more snow."

"Go and hitch the buggy for her, then."

"You weren't going to have her walk, were you?"

Her mother put her hands on her hips. "I've made this now and I'm not going to have it go to waste."

"You're really going to send her out in this weather?" he asked.

"I haven't cooked all day for nothing. Either she's walking over there in the snow, or she's going in the buggy. You choose which one."

Her father stood up and murmured, "I better go and hitch the buggy."

Marlene and Matthew were up in their room because Marlene was upset about something.

"I'll just go upstairs and put some warmer clothes on," Grace said to her mother once her father had walked outside. Once in her room, Grace pulled a second pair of black stockings on. Then she changed into her warmest dress, and placed her over-bonnet over the top of her prayer *kapp*. When she came downstairs, her mother was waiting by the front door.

"Now tell him you cooked it," she said holding out a basket that contained a large saucepan.

There was no use arguing with her mother when she was in one of those moods. Even her father had backed down about Grace going out in such bad weather.

After wrapping herself in a heavy cape, Grace took the basket from her mother's hands and waited until she saw her father driving the horse and buggy out of the barn. She felt sorry for the horse leaving his warm stable, and she also felt sorry for herself. Snow was falling lightly.

When Grace was halfway to Adam's house, the snow began to fall more heavily. Looking back in the direction of her house, and then looking toward Adam's, she decided to keep going.

She pulled her horse up under the cover of Adam's barn. When she stepped down, she saw Adam at his door. He placed something over his head and ran to her.

As soon as he was under cover with her, he lowered the blanket. "What are you doing, Grace?"

"My *mudder* had a crazy idea that you needed some food," she said.

"Well, that's not so crazy. Where is it – did you bring it with you?"

"In the back."

He pulled the food out of the back and covered them both with the blanket. "I hope you're going to join me."

"I will. I'm not going home right now in this," she answered.

"You cover us with the blanket. I'll hold the food, and we'll make a run for it."

Once she had the blanket over the both of them, they made a dash for the house.

He shut the door behind them with a backward flick of his foot. "Just drop the blanket on the floor there, then stand in front of the fire!" he ordered.

She walked over to the fire and warmed her back until she had thawed enough to take her cape off. She threw her cape over a chair and then walked into the kitchen to join Adam. "It's nice and warm in your *haus*."

"I'm just heating up the food."

"We shouldn't be together like this, Adam."

He took his eyes off the stove and studied her face. "What do you mean?"

"Alone, just the two of us."

"I think the snow has other ideas about that. Besides, Aunt Sarah is upstairs asleep. She's just been awake for two days straight delivering one of the Wilsons' babies. So, we're not entirely alone."

Grace smiled and nodded, wondering whether

Adam thought she was silly to be worried about what people might think.

He took the lid off the pot and smelled the chicken casserole. "Mmm, this smells delicious. You are eating, aren't you?"

Grace pulled a chair out and sat down at the kitchen table. "I am."

"It shouldn't take too long to heat up. Did you make it?"

"I didn't, but I'm supposed to tell you that I did."

Adam laughed. "Did your *mudder* make it?"

"*Jah*, she did." Grace had already lied about the buggy – she didn't want to add to her list of deceptions by lying to him about the food as well. "Does Sarah often stay here?"

"She does when she's been working nearby and she's too tired to make the trip home."

"We should save some food for her."

"There's enough for two families – I'm sure we can manage to leave her some."

When they heard the contents of the saucepan bubbling on the stove, Adam rose from his chair. "Sounds like it's ready. I hope I haven't burnt it." Adam dished out two bowls of food and sat down again.

They both said silent prayers of thanks for the food.

"Have you grown used to the idea that you're going to be a *mudder?*"

Grace shook her head. "Not yet."

"Can I ask you what your husband was like? I'll understand if you don't want to talk about it."

Grace finished chewing her mouthful. "You can ask me anything. It started out okay; I mean, I thought I was in love with him. I don't know if I was or if I liked all the attention he was giving me. I was upset over what had happened between you and me."

"And he wasted no time in moving in and taking advantage of you."

Grace raised her eyebrows.

"I'm sorry. It's not my business to say such things."

"It wasn't a good marriage. We argued all the time, and he tried to control me. He wouldn't allow me to have friends unless they were his friends. Nothing I did was ever good enough. I can't tell you more than that. It would make me too upset."

"I didn't know it was like that. I had no idea."

"He treated me badly and the worst thing was, he acted differently to everyone else. Jeremy was so nice to other people that no one would've known he treated me so badly. He even tried to strangle me, and only stopped himself at the last minute." Grace's fingertips touched her neck. "I had bruises on my neck for weeks."

"Grace, why did you stay with him for so long?"

"He wasn't always mean. Sometimes he'd be really nice. After he was horrible to me he'd apologize and say he'd never do it again. I thought sometimes that he was improving. Anyway, when I'd had enough, I told him I was leaving and that's when he flew into a rage and pressed his hands around my neck until I fell to the floor."

Adam stared at her in disbelief. He shook his head. "That's terrible. I wish you'd come to me and told me. You've had a hard time of it."

Grace nodded. "I didn't want to give up on my marriage. I had it in my mind that marriage was forever. Divorce or even separation was never an option."

"What had you planned to do, then? After you told him you'd had enough? Come back to the community, and never marry? Because you wouldn't have been able to marry if you were divorced."

"I hadn't thought that far ahead. All I knew was that I couldn't be with him any more."

"I can understand that, and with him not being a believer, he'd have no reason to keep working on the marriage."

Grace nodded. "That's true. And what about you, have you come close to marriage?"

He shook his head. "I've not come close to it. I had thought at one point that you and I might be heading toward it, but then things happened."

"There are lots of young women in the community. Aren't any of them suitable?"

Adam laughed. "I don't think so."

Grace smiled at him and took another sip of her hot chocolate. "So not one woman has sparked your interest?" She had to find out. Maybe he would say that she'd been the only woman he'd ever been interested in.

"There was one woman after you, if you're forcing me to be truthful. The year after you left the community; we got along really well and then she suddenly left just like you did."

"Is she someone I know?"

"Not likely. Her name's Ida Schwartz. I've learned not to plan too far ahead because sometimes unexpected things happen, and things don't work out. It leads to disappointment."

"You mean when things don't turn out how you thought they would?"

"That's right."

"I guess we never know what's going to happen, do we? We had the last meeting at the Schwartzes' house. Mr. and Mrs. Schwartz are Ida's parents?"

"That's right."

Grace nodded and wondered why Marlene hadn't once made mention of Ida.

Sarah woke up some time after Grace and Adam had eaten and was pleased to have Mrs. Byler's food to eat. Then the three of them sat and drank hot chocolate in the living room. The snow was still falling heavily, so Grace stayed the night in the room adjacent to the one Sarah was in.

∾

THREE WEEKS LATER, after a Sunday meeting, Grace was one of three people who were baptized.

"Let's get you home now," her mother said putting her arm around her shoulders. "It's too cold to be out in this."

When they started walking to the buggy, Grace stopped and stared at Adam who was some distance away. "Who is that old man Adam's talking with?"

"That's Noah Schwartz, Ida's *vadder.* They're probably speaking about Ida coming back to the community."

"Ida's coming back to the community?"

"*Jah,* did you know her? Or had you left by the time they moved here?"

"Wasn't Adam close to Ida before she left the community? That's what I've heard."

"That's right. I'm sorry, Grace. I completely forgot that he and Ida were close."

She knew by her mother's tone that she thought there was no hope of her and Adam ever being married if Ida came back to the community.

Grace said to her mother, "Okay, we'd better get out of this cold." They hurried toward the buggy. Grace would just concentrate on her baby and forget about Adam as much as she possibly could.

CHAPTER 14

My little children, these things write I unto you, that ye sin not And if any man sin, we have an advocate with the Father, Jesus Christ the righteous:
1 John 2:1

THE NEXT DAY she walked over to Adam's house, glad that the snow wasn't falling. She'd been doing chores for him nearly every day for the past three weeks. He waved to her and she walked over to him.

"You don't have to keep coming here. My place has never been so clean. I think you've paid off the debt by now."

Was that true, or did he not want Ida to see that the two of them had become close? "It keeps me out of *Mamm* and Marlene's way, so I don't mind. They're bottling preserves and jams every day. They've opened a small stall at the farmers market."

"That will keep Marlene busy."

"*Jah*, and Matthew's pleased for the extra money."

He dusted off his hands. "Come in and I'll make you a cup of tea. I feel awful that you've done so much around this place."

"Don't feel bad. It was *Dat* who forced me to do it. I mean, I wanted to do it to pay off my debts. It was a silly thing to do."

"*Jah*, it was. It was the kind of thing Marlene would do." He stared at her and raised an eyebrow.

Grace frowned. "I suppose."

"Let's go." Adam strode toward the house.

"You're not working today?" She'd heard from Matthew that he was taking a day off.

"*Jah*, I'm having a rest today. I take a day off every couple of weeks besides Sunday. Other than that, I work six days a week. Come sit by the fire." He opened the door for her to walk inside. He pulled two chairs closer to the fire. "There you go; have a seat."

He returned a few minutes later with hot chocolate. After he passed her a mug, he sat and took a mouthful of his hot drink. He looked across at her. "You're not sick, are you?"

Grace laughed. "I haven't been sick for a few weeks now; hopefully that's behind me." Grace took a sip of her hot chocolate. "I heard that Ida is coming back to the community." She said it as casually as she could.

"*Jah*, her *vadder* told me yesterday she's back and she's going to be baptized."

"That's good. We need more women in the community."

"She's a lot like you, you know."

Grace raised her eyebrows. "How's she like me?"

"She's a calming person to be around, just like you. I've probably never said this to you, but you have a calming effect on me."

Grace took a sip of hot chocolate. She realized he might have been spending time working on his buggy so he could take Ida out in it. She couldn't control the pangs of jealousy that gnawed at her insides.

All of a sudden Adam laughed.

She looked at him. "What's so funny?"

He shook his head. "I was waiting until you told me yourself, but since you haven't I need to tell you that I know it was Marlene driving that buggy and not you. I watched the whole thing from my window. I heard my horse take off and I ran outside. I can see that part of the road from my upstairs bedroom. I saw you galloping along after the buggy." He shook his head. "I don't know what you were trying to do."

"You saw it?"

"Most of it. As soon as the buggy tipped over, I ran as fast as I could."

"Why didn't you say anything? You've had me coming over here and doing all this work when all the time you knew it wasn't me?" *Are all men deceptive like*

Jeremy? "Why did you have me think that you thought I did it?"

"Don't be mad at me. It felt nice coming home knowing you'd been here."

She shook her head at him.

He added, "If you weren't doing chores here you'd only be doing them at home. Besides, you were being deceptive telling me it was you who damaged my buggy."

"I suppose you've got me there."

"I'll make it up to you, Grace. I will. I was certain Marlene would say something soon."

Grace shrugged. "I do feel a bit sorry for her sometimes. She feels a little bit isolated and the odd one out in the house. And she also didn't want Matthew to be cranky with her. She's just going through a hard time at the moment. Like we all do sometimes."

"You're a very caring woman, Grace."

"Sometimes," she said with a smile.

"You're very honest."

"Not so honest. I didn't tell you the truth about the buggy."

Just when she thought he was going to say something about seeing her again or maybe taking her on a date, he leaped to his feet. "Well, finish up and I'll take you back home."

"I can walk; I need the exercise."

"You don't need to walk in this cold. I'll take you home. I'm going out anyway so it's not a problem."

Grace finished the last mouthful and Adam put his hand out to take the cup from her.

"Now that I've made my confession to you about the buggy, I'll think of a way to make it up to you," he said.

"It doesn't matter. I'm the one who's lied to everybody telling them I damaged your buggy, so why don't we call it even?"

"*Nee.*" He shook his head. "I'll make it up to you, Grace. I won't have you doing all that hard work for nothing."

As Grace followed him out to the buggy she wondered whether Adam wanted to see her again or whether he just didn't want to feel indebted to her. He was so hard to read sometimes.

After he'd taken her home, she told her mother that she wasn't going to clean Adam's house anymore because he'd refused her help.

Her mother was pleased that she would now be helping her and Marlene make the jams and preserves.

When Grace's mother went out of the kitchen for a couple of minutes, Marlene whispered to Grace, "The girl Adam likes is back in the community. Her name's Ida and she's really pretty."

"I heard about Ida coming back. It'll be good to have an extra woman in the community, won't it?" Grace fixed a smile on her face.

"You can't fool me. I know you can't possibly be happy about that. I know you like Adam."

"I can't do anything about that. I've got no control over Adam, or what he does. I just have to concentrate on my *boppli*."

"*Jah*, I suppose that's a good idea. Forget about Adam and when you have your *boppli* you might meet someone else."

Grace's mother came back into the room. "Who's going to meet someone else?"

"Grace is. We were just taking about Adam."

"Of course you'll meet someone else, Grace."

"Why don't we talk about something other than Adam?" Grace asked.

"We'll talk about something else, then," her mother said. "Haven't you got an appointment at the midwife's house tomorrow?"

"*Jah*, Matthew's driving me there. It's at four in the afternoon."

"*Gut.*"

"Your tummy's poking out a bit now," Marlene said, pointing at Grace's stomach.

"*Jah*, you can see you're expecting now," Grace's mother said.

Grace looked down at her tummy and smiled. "He's growing bigger."

"He's a boy?" Marlene asked.

Grace shrugged. "I don't know. I feel that he might be a boy, but I don't mind if he turns out to be a girl. I have to have an ultrasound soon. I might be able to find out but I don't want to."

Marlene changed the subject entirely. "I'm glad you came up with the idea for me to make these preserves and jams, Grace."

"I'm happy that you like making them, and selling them."

"It's given us something to do, hasn't it, *Mamm*?"

Grace's mother chuckled. "I had enough to do before, but I do enjoy it." They were sharing a stall at the farmers market with other people. Their day was Thursday, and they spent the week getting the goods prepared.

CHAPTER 15.

Repent ye therefore, and be converted,
that your sins may be blotted out,
when the times of refreshing shall come from
the presence of the Lord;
Acts 3:19

Grace was working in the kitchen with Marlene and her mother when they heard hoofbeats outside.

Marlene ran to the window. "It's Ida and her *mudder.*"

"Quick, Grace, put the pot on to boil," her mother said. "Marlene, clean up while I take them into the living room. I hope they don't come into the kitchen. Quick girls, hurry."

Grace's mother hurried out of the kitchen and the two girls giggled.

"I wonder why they're here," Marlene said.

"Is this the first time they've come?"

"*Nee.* Mrs. Schwartz has visited before."

Grace and Marlene cleaned up the kitchen while Mrs. Byler greeted Ida and her mother and sat them in the living room, and as soon as the two girls had finished cleaning up the kitchen, they joined them there.

Grace's mother looked up. "Come over here, Grace. I want you to meet Ida.

Grace and Ida greeted one another, and then Grace said, "I haven't met you yet, Mrs. Schwartz. I left before you arrived in the community."

Grace's mother called Marlene over. "Sit down next to me, Marlene. You've met Ida, haven't you?"

Marlene smiled and sat down. "*Jah.* I met Ida before. It's nice to see you back here."

"*Denke*, Marlene. I'm happy to be back."

"I just wanted Ida to come over here and meet you girls. The friends she had aren't here anymore for one reason or another. I thought she should meet some girls her own age. You don't mind me stopping by?"

"I'm glad you've come over," Mrs. Byler said. "We just finished bottling preserves. We sell them one day a week at the farmers market on a Thursday. That's what Marlene and I do."

Ida looked over at Grace. "And what do you do?"

"Not much. I'm just about to have a baby in a couple months." Grace patted her stomach.

Ida said, "That's right, I heard someone mention that. I'm sorry to hear about your husband."

"*Jah,* but it's *gut* now that you're back in the community among your *familye* and your friends," Mrs. Schwartz said.

Grace nodded and smiled. As Ida talked to Marlene, Grace studied her. What man wouldn't think Ida was attractive with her light-colored hair, blue eyes and even-toned skin?

"You should come to my quilting bee. The three of you should come," Mrs. Schwartz said. "We have it on Wednesday mornings. Would you like to come along, girls?"

"*Jah*, that will give me something to do," Grace said.

"And when is your *boppli* due, Grace?" Ida asked.

"In a couple of months. I'm not really sure of the dates." She looked down and held her tummy with both hands. "This little one was a bit of a surprise. I didn't find out until my husband had passed away, and..." Her voice trailed away. She didn't want to tell everybody that the baby wasn't planned. News like that had a way of traveling and Grace didn't want her baby to hear of anything negative when she or he got older.

"Don't worry, you won't be alone forever. You're still young," Mrs. Schwartz said. Then she turned to Marlene. "Isn't it time you had *kinner* yourself, Marlene?"

Grace looked at Marlene and hoped she wasn't

going to cry. Marlene pressed her lips together and said, "*Jah*, it will be my turn next if *Gott* wills it."

"All in His timing," Grace's mother said. "Now who would like tea?

Marlene jumped up. "I'll get it." Without waiting for anybody to respond, Marlene walked quickly towards the kitchen.

Grace knew why Marlene was upset, so she stood up and left the room to help her. She found Marlene in the kitchen, putting the pot on the stove and fighting back tears.

Grace put her hands on Marlene's shoulders. "I don't like to see you upset like this, Marlene."

"I'll be okay; there's nothing you can do about it anyway."

Grace had no idea what to say. It didn't help when people pointed out that she'd been married for years and there was no baby on the horizon.

Marlene said, "You go out and talk to Ida. I'm all right in here."

"Are you sure?"

Marlene nodded. Grace hadn't wanted to leave Ida with the two older women, especially since she'd come specifically so she could talk to Grace and Marlene. Grace returned to the living room.

"You'd know Adam very well, wouldn't you Marlene, since you've lived next door to him all your life?" Mrs. Schwartz asked.

Grace gave a little giggle. "I'm not Marlene, I'm Grace."

Mrs. Schwartz laughed. "I'm sorry. I find it hard to remember names."

"*Jah.* I've known him my whole life, but I didn't see him in the four years I was away."

Mrs. Schwartz continued, "And why do you think he's never married?"

She felt everybody's eyes on her. "I'm not sure; he's never mentioned anything to me about it. We're not that close that he would tell me all his secrets."

"You're not close?" Ida asked.

"Not at all. I mean, we're friends, that's what we are, I suppose." She looked at her mother, hoping she'd change the subject. It was clear that Ida and her mother weren't there to get to know Marlene and Grace at all. They were simply there to gather information about Adam, hoping he was still available and wasn't seeing anyone.

Marlene came out at the right time with a pot of tea and teacups on a tray.

Grace's mother said, "Marlene, why don't you get the blueberry cake out and cut it up into slices?"

"Good idea. I forgot we had that. I mean, it's fresh – we only made it yesterday."

Ida and her mother laughed.

The rest of their visit was spent talking about quilting. They all agreed to go to Mrs. Schwartz's quilting bee on Wednesday morning.

When they left, Marlene and Grace got the dinner ready while Grace's mother sipped on another cup of tea in the living room.

"Why do people mention *kinner* to me all the time, Grace? Why?"

"I suppose many people don't know what else to talk about. They could be doing nothing more than making conversation."

"How do you feel about Ida, Grace?"

"She seems very nice."

Marlene nodded and said no more.

As Grace plunged her hands into the dishwashing water, she said, "There's nothing I can do about it."

"So you do like Adam?"

"Of course I like Adam. He's a good friend." Grace wasn't ready to trust Marlene with the secrets in her heart.

"I won't tell anybody. If I know you like him, I can help you."

Grace laughed. "If things are going to happen between us they'll happen without interference. Ida seems nice. Maybe she and Adam will get married." Grace shrugged her shoulders and handed Marlene a plate to dry.

"Your *mudder* said I'd find you girls in here."

Both girls swung around to see who belonged to the male voice behind them. It was Adam, and Grace only hoped that he hadn't heard what she'd just said.

"Who am I supposed to be getting married to?"

Marlene giggled, and said, "You tell him, Grace."

Grace felt her face flush with warmth. "It's nothing. We were just gossiping; sometimes girls do that. Have a seat at the table and I'll make you a cup of tea. We've just boiled the pot."

"It looks like I just missed out on seeing Ida and her *mudder*. I saw them driving off as I was walking over. You think Ida and I will marry, Grace?"

Grace's mouth fell open and she was frozen to the spot while Marlene threw her tea-towel down and sat at the kitchen table opposite Adam.

Marlene said, "Everyone knows you were dating before she left the community."

Grace found her voice. "Marlene! Those things are private and should not be discussed." Grace passed her the tea towel and said, "Finish wiping up and I'll make Adam a cup of tea."

"I hope that's not too much trouble. It'll be giving you another cup to clean," Adam said.

"No trouble at all. What's *Mamm* doing in the living room?"

Adam said, "When I came through the front door she was nearly asleep."

"You walked here?" Marlene asked.

"I did, since I've still got one buggy out of operation."

Grace and Adam stared at Marlene who silently continued drying the dishes. They exchanged glances, knowing that they'd have to wait longer for Marlene to confess that it was she who ran Adam's buggy off the road.

Grace made three cups of hot tea and set one in front of Adam. She placed one out for Marlene, and sat down with one herself. "I'll let *Mamm* have a rest in the living room. She's only just had a cup of tea; I doubt she'll want another."

"I just remembered I had something to do upstairs. I'll take my tea with me." Marlene made herself scarce, leaving Adam and Grace alone in the kitchen.

"How long do you think it's going to be before she tells the truth?" Adam asked.

Grace laughed. "Sometime between now and never; maybe closer to never."

Adam took a sip of tea and Grace wondered if he was there to say something to her.

Finally he spoke. "You and the *boppli* have been good?"

"*Jah*, your Aunt Sarah has been looking after us well."

He nodded. "That's good news. I wanted to tell you something, Grace, now that we're alone."

Grace stared at him and had a sip of tea while waiting to hear what he was going to say.

"I mentioned to you that Ida and I had a close relationship before she left the community."

Grace nodded, knowing what was coming next. When he hesitated, Grace said, "It's fine. You don't need to explain anything to me."

"I don't want you to get the wrong idea."

"I think I know what you're trying to say, Adam."

"I'm not certain that you do. I just wanted to say that it's you…"

Grace's mother stepped into the kitchen, interrupting them. "Where's Marlene?"

"She's gone up to her bedroom. Would you like more tea, *Mamm?*"

"I think I'd like *kaffe.*" Grace's mother sat down at the kitchen table next to Adam while Grace got her a cup of coffee. "We just had visitors. Ida and her *mudder* were here. I thought they might have gone to visit you after they called here to see us."

"I'm not certain. Maybe they did, but I came here on foot through the fields. I did see their buggy heading down the road."

"You must be pleased she's back," Mrs. Byler said to Adam.

"Milk, *mudder?*"

"*Nee.*" Mrs. Byler swung around to stare at her. "You know I never have milk, Grace."

"Would you like some cake, Adam?"

"*Jah*, I would."

Grace sat back down at the table, passed her mother a cup of coffee, and then pushed the plate of cake along to Adam. He chewed on a mouthful of cake while her mother told him how sorry she was that Grace had damaged his buggy so badly.

"Don't worry about that, Mrs. Byler. That's all been

sorted out now. Matthew is helping me fix it, and Grace has paid me off by doing chores."

"*Jah*, there's no need to mention it again, *Mamm*."

"And what brings you here today, Adam? Were you hoping that Matthew would be home?"

"*Nee*. I knew Matthew would be at work at this time. I came to speak to Grace."

"About the buggy?" Mrs. Byler asked.

Adam leaned back with his huge smile on his face. "*Nee*, not about the buggy. We're forgetting about the buggy. We've moved past the buggy ordeal."

All of a sudden, Grace couldn't face knowing why he was there. She thought he might have been about to say that he liked her, and as much as she wanted that to be true, she was too filled with mixed emotions to hear what he had to say.

"Can our talk wait, Adam? I'm really tired right now."

Adam sprang to his feet. "Is there anything I can do?"

She shook her head. "I need to lie down."

Her mother said, "Are you sure you're all right, Grace? You've come over all pale and ill-looking."

"I'm fine." Grace walked out of the room and climbed the stairs to her bedroom, closing the bedroom door behind her. She lay down and had a rest while wondering if she should've stayed to let Adam finish speaking.

With Ida, Adam would have a chance to start a

family since Ida had never married. Surely Adam's life would be less complicated with Ida. But what if he'd come to say that he'd liked her and not Ida? If that were the case, he'd had plenty of opportunities to say so.

There was a quiet knock on her door and before she could speak, the door creaked open.

"Are you asleep?" Marlene hissed.

"*Nee.* Come in." Grace rolled on her side and pushed herself up. Then she leaned against the wall that her bed was pushed against.

"I can hear every word in the kitchen from my bedroom. He nearly admitted he was here to talk to you. Why did you leave before he could say anything to you?"

"It's just complicated. I feel overwhelmed with so many things right at the moment. Everything is unknown for me. When I first married Jeremy, I thought everything would be wonderful but the next few years had so many ups and downs – it was just awful. And look at me now; I'm pregnant without a *vadder* for my *boppli* and I'm living back at my parents' *haus.*"

"You have to be patient, Grace. Isn't your mother always saying that things happen in *Gott's* timing?"

"I think I am being patient. Even if Adam had said he likes me, I'm not ready for any more changes in my life right now."

"You have to be patient with yourself. Once your child is born and things get back to normal, then you can decide what you want to do. Even get a job and get your own place if you don't want to live here forever. Or you could live with Matthew and me when we get a home."

"*Denke*, Marlene. That's a very nice offer. I'll keep that in mind."

"He might have been going to ask you to marry him. That's the only thing that makes sense. If he liked Ida, wouldn't he have tried to wave their buggy down to talk to them? He didn't seem the least concerned that they might be going to his house when your mother said that might be what they had in mind."

"I'm almost too scared to think that it might be true. I'm not used to good things happening to me. I just want to keep away from everybody and go into a dark cave, a quiet dark cave."

"Anyway, now we've got a quilting bee to go to."

Grace nodded. "I'll enjoy that. I haven't been to one for ages. I'll make one for my baby."

"I've got lots of material you can have. I've been collecting it for when I have a *boppli*. You can have whatever you want. I've got so many nice colors: soft yellows, greens, blues, and apricot."

"*Denke*, but don't you want to save them for when your time comes?"

"I've got more than enough for six quilts." Marlene giggled. "When I first got married I'd go to the store nearly every week and buy fabric until Matthew told me I was spending too much money. That's the bad thing about being married; you have to consider the other person and what they want." Marlene stood. "I'll let you have a sleep and when you wake up we can have a look at the material together."

"*Denke*, Marlene. I'd really like that."

When Marlene left the room, Grace thought on what she'd said about compromise. There hadn't been any compromise in her marriage to Jeremy. Jeremy was the one who called all the shots; it had been his way or no way at all.

When Grace opened her eyes, she saw by the sun out the window that was late afternoon. She got out of bed and hurried down the stairs to help with the dinner.

"Grace, you shouldn't be rushing about like that when you're so large," her mother said.

"I just didn't want you to fix dinner on your own."

"Nonsense. Marlene's helping."

"*Mamm*, can Grace and I disappear for a few minutes?"

"I'll need you to peel the vegetables in fifteen minutes."

"I'm going to show Grace all the fabric I've got. She's going to choose some to make a quilt."

"That's a *wunderbaar* idea. I'll help you with that quilt, Grace. We'll get it done that much faster that way."

"That will be lovely."

When the two girls went upstairs to Marlene's

room, Grace was surprised how many boxes there were stacked against the side of the wall. "You don't have much room to move in here."

"I've got a lot of things for my house already. There's nowhere else to put them."

"I'll help you take them to one of the spare rooms."

"Your *mudder* said she wants them free for when guests come."

"When was the last time we had people stay overnight?"

"About six months ago."

"Surely we can leave them in a room and then move them when someone comes?"

"That's what I suggested and your *mudder* said no. I told you I don't feel very welcome here."

"You *are* welcome. I guess *Mamm's* just got her funny ways." Grace shrugged.

"Now, I'm not sure what box the materials are in." Marlene started opening the boxes and placing them in the middle of the floor when they weren't what she was looking for. "Here, this box." She opened the box and pulled each piece of material out.

"I can't choose. They're all so lovely. Why don't you take what you want first, Marlene? I don't want to take anything that you might want."

"Grace, I might never have *kinner*. There's obviously something wrong with me. Maybe *Gott* is punishing me."

"I don't think *Gott* punishes."

"Ever heard of Job? Look at all the horrible things that happened to him."

"*Jah*, but that was in the Old Testament and now we're under the new. And remember, Job was being tested, not punished"

"I'm not so sure about that."

"From what I recall it says in the Bible that the rain falls on both the just and the unjust, meaning bad things can happen to everyone."

Marlene nodded. "I thought when I got baptized and married everything would be perfect in my life."

"And I thought when I got married to Jeremy we'd be happily married and grow old together."

"Your marriage to Jeremy wasn't in *Gott's* plan for you, though, because he was an *Englischer.*"

"I'm just saying we don't know what life holds for us because we're not in control. All we can do is cope the best with what happens to us. I didn't ask for Jeremy to treat me badly, and then die. I didn't ask to be pregnant and have to be a single parent, but all these things have happened."

"But that all brought you back to the community, Grace. Most of it did. So I can see that might have been in His plan for you, but what sense does it make for me to have no *kinner*?"

"I don't know the answer. But what you said isn't right – I was coming back anyway. I'd told Jeremy I was leaving him just before he died. There was no reason for him to die. As horrible as he was to me sometimes, I didn't want him to die."

Marlene raised her eyebrows. "I didn't know you were leaving him."

"I made the decision I didn't want to be married to him anymore."

"You mean you were going to divorce?"

"I don't know if I would have divorced him or not. I was going to separate from him."

"And then you could never marry again if Jeremy was still alive."

"That didn't matter to me. I'd much rather he still be alive somewhere even though it would mean that I could never marry again. Well, I could marry, but not if I came back to the community."

"You can marry again now – you're free." Marlene's gaze fell to the fabric laid out on the bed. "You take your pick, Grace."

Grace chose soft yellows and blues.

CHAPTER 15

*In whom we have redemption through his blood, the
forgiveness of sins,
according to the riches of his grace;*
Ephesians 1:7

FOR THE PAST WEEKS, Grace had avoided Adam because
she was scared of what he'd say. Marlene and her
mother had taken over the making of the baby's quilt
and now it was finished and waiting in the crib.

It was early morning when Grace stepped out of
bed. Warm water gushed from her and made a puddle
on the floor. She knew her waters had broken and
she'd soon be getting labor pains. She couldn't stop
herself from screaming.

She stepped over the puddle, opened her door, and

yelled, "*Mamm*, my water just broke!" She could hear her mother running down the hallway towards her. Grace held her nightgown up.

"We'll have to tell Sarah." Her mother yelled over her shoulder at Marlene to call the midwife from the phone in the barn.

"You change out of these clothes and I'll get the room ready." Her mother set about gathering clean towels and sheets.

"I'm not having any pain yet, *Mamm*," Grace said when her mother came back into her room.

"You will."

"Some people don't have much pain. I might be one of those people."

"It's not likely," her mother said.

Unfortunately her mother was right. By the time the midwife arrived two hours later, Grace was in a lot of pain. "Make them stop..."

Marlene was wiping her head with a wet washcloth while the midwife examined her.

"Not long to go; you're already nearly fully dilated."

"You can do this, Grace. You don't have long to go," Marlene said.

Grace's thoughts turned to Jeremy. Would he have been pleased about becoming a father? With Jeremy, it was hard to know what he thought about anything; he was so unpredictable and unstable. He was the total opposite of Adam.

Another wave of contractions crunched her body.

When they left, she said, "I didn't know it was going to be this bad."

The midwife said, "Walk around. Sometimes that eases the contractions."

"*Nee*, I'm too big to get up. I want to stay in bed."

"You can stay in bed," her mother said. "It's all right. You don't have to get out of bed."

Her mother was speaking to her as though she were a child. And Marlene was annoying her by constantly dabbing the washcloth on her forehead.

"How much longer do you think it's going to be?" her mother asked the midwife.

"Why, *Mamm*? Have you somewhere else you want to be?"

Her mother stared at her. "I don't like seeing you in all this pain."

"It's best if we don't call it pain," the midwife said.

Her mother looked down and kept silent.

Ten minutes later, the contractions stopped and then there was nothing. Grace felt she didn't know what to do with herself. All she knew was that she couldn't go on. "I need to go get a cesarean. They'll have to cut it out. I can't do it anymore."

"Sounds like you're in transition. You're most likely ready to push." After a brief examination, she said, "You're fully dilated."

"I don't feel like pushing!" Grace heard herself scream.

"You will soon," both her mother and the midwife said at the same time.

She grabbed the washcloth that Marlene kept dabbing her forehead with and threw it across the room.

"Maybe try and sit up a little. The force of gravity on the baby's head might hurry things along," Sarah said.

They all helped Grace sit up. She had to roll onto her side and then sit up from there.

"I might be able to walk a little," Grace said.

As soon as she stood, she had the urge to push.

Three quarters of an hour later, her baby was born. It was a girl.

The midwife immediately examined the baby, and then she wrapped her in a white cotton sheet and handed her to Grace. Grace looked down at the miracle in her arms and tears of joy streamed down her face. This was her miracle baby, and she was so perfect in every way.

"Have you thought of a name, Grace?" her mother asked.

"Only boys' names."

"She's my first niece," Marlene said.

Grace couldn't stop staring at the small bundle in her arms. An overwhelming feeling of love for her baby swept over her. She kissed her baby on her nearly-bald head, and then breathed in the fresh smell of the newborn.

Marlene hadn't stopped peering over her shoulder. "I'll give you a chance to hold her in a minute, Marlene."

"I'd like that more than anything."

Minutes later, Marlene was the first person to hold the baby.

"She's just so tiny. I didn't know she'd be this small."

Small? Grace was immediately concerned. "Is she meant to be so small?" Grace asked the midwife.

"She's not so tiny. I'd say she'd be around seven pounds. I've got my scales in the buggy – I can weigh her later."

"And she's all healthy and everything?" Grace asked.

"She's perfectly fine and healthy. I'll stop in every day for the next week to check on both of you. That was very fast for a first birth, Grace."

"It was?"

Sarah nodded, and then Sarah and Grace's mother cleaned up the room while Marlene and Grace took turns of holding the baby.

THAT EVENING, when Grace's father and Matthew came home, they fussed over the baby. Grace could see that Marlene's longing for a baby of her own was making her increasingly upset.

"I'll bring dinner up to you," Marlene announced as she hurried out of the room by herself. While her father was across the room holding the baby, her mother beside him talking to her newest granddaughter, Grace whispered to Matthew, "Go and see that she's all right. I think she's a little upset and it doesn't help seeing everyone fussing over the *boppli*."

Matthew rolled his eyes. "She's always upset about one thing or another."

"That is so awful. You know she wants a baby and it can't be easy for her that I've got one without trying. Can't you see that that would make her upset?"

"*Nee*, not really. It'll be better to have one when we're in our own home anyway. We don't need one right now when we're still trying to save for a home."

"Just talk to her and be nice. Why are you so horrible sometimes?"

"Okay." Matthew rolled his eyes and walked out the door.

"What was that about, Grace? Is Marlene upset?" her mother asked.

"You know how sensitive she is about having a *boppli*. I was just telling Matthew that you should all be more sensitive toward her."

"You're right, Grace. You've always been a sensible girl. We'll be more understanding," her father said. "Now, what will we call this little girl?"

"I don't know. Something will come to me sooner or later."

"You should call her Beth after my *grossmammi*; that's a fine name," her father said.

"Or what about Faith after my *mudder?*"

"*Nee*, I want something more unusual than that."

"Faith is an unusual name. I don't know of any other people called Faith apart from my *mudder.*"

"I think I might call her a flower name. Maybe Lilly, or Daisy."

Her father added, "Rhododendron, or how about Geranium?"

Grace and her mother laughed.

"I won't be calling her Rhododendron."

Her father passed the baby back to her.

Grace looked down at her baby. "I want to call her a happy name."

"What about Joy? That's a happy name," her father said.

"Yes, I like it. *Denke, Dat.* Her name is Joy. Joy Stevens."

"Aren't you going back to using Byler?" her father asked.

"*Nee.* I think the she should have my last name. We're on a journey together. Part of our journey was Jeremy, so we'll keep his name.

"Well, I hope your journey doesn't take you too far from here," her father said with a laugh. "You're welcome to stay with us forever."

"I know I am, but someday we'll have to make our own way in the world."

"Grace, where did you get that thinking from? We're a family and we remain together. Your brothers and sisters have all married so when your *vadder* and I are old you can have this *haus* to yourself. We'll build a *grossdawdi haus* on."

Her father looked at his wife. "We will?"

She nodded. "*Jah.*"

He raised his eyebrows and smiled. "I'm not in the mood to disagree with your *mudder.*"

She was grateful to her parents, but they were speaking as though she'd never marry again. Her baby deserved to have a father, a male figure in her life, and she wanted to experience a proper husband who loved her and cared for her. She wanted to experience that at least once in her life.

"I'll go down and see what's happened to Marlene and Matthew," her mother said.

Her mother and father walked out of the room and for the first time she was alone with her baby. She placed her on the bed beside her.

"Let's have a rest before dinner," she whispered.

She closed her eyes and said a prayer of thanks that her baby was safe and healthy.

CHAPTER 16

*If we confess our sins, he is faithful and just to forgive us our
sins, and to cleanse us from all unrighteousness.*
1 John 1:9

THE NEXT MORNING, Grace came downstairs with baby
Joy in her arms.

Her mother walked out of the kitchen. "Grace, you
can stay in bed for a few days."

"*Nee.* I feel fine and I'd bet you didn't rest after you
had a *boppli.*"

"We don't 'bet' on anything, Grace. You mustn't say
that again."

"I didn't mean to say it. I won't say it again." She was
a grown woman who was being treated like a child and

that probably wouldn't change while she was living in her parents' home.

"*Gut*! I had too many *kinner* to look after to have a rest," she chuckled. "You go and sit on the couch and I'll bring your breakfast out on a tray."

"*Denke, Mamm.*" Grace wasn't used to getting spoiled, but she wasn't going to complain about it.

A few minutes later, Marlene and Matthew came down the stairs. Marlene walked right into the kitchen without looking at her. Grace wondered if Matthew and Marlene had just had an argument.

"Good morning, Grace and Joy," Matthew said brightly.

He leaned over, stared at the baby, and then made his way into the kitchen just as Grace's mother was bringing a tray of breakfast out to her.

"I'm being spoiled," Grace said.

"All first-time *mudders* should be spoiled every now and again," Grace's mother said.

They heard a knock at the door and her mother swung to face it. "I think that'll be a visitor for you."

"Me?" Grace straightened up in case the visitor was Adam. When her mother opened the door, she saw that it was.

"I've heard that there's a new *boppli* in the *haus*."

Grace's mother laughed. "There certainly is, and you'll never see a cuter one."

Adam walked in further and Grace smiled at him. "Here she is."

He walked over and kneeled down to have a closer look. "She's perfect."

"I've called her Joy."

"She'll bring you Joy." He looked down at Grace's breakfast. "I hope I'm not interrupting your meal."

"*Nee*, you're not, Adam. Have you eaten?" her mother asked.

"I have, Mrs. Byler. I just wanted to call in. Aunt Sarah stayed at my *haus* rather than going all the way home last night and she told me the news."

"She could've stayed here; we've got plenty of spare bedrooms," Mrs. Byler said.

"She's got her own room at my house because she lives so far away," Adam explained before he turned back to Grace.

Grace heard her mother mutter under her breath before she went into the kitchen, "Well, she only needed to ask."

"And how are you feeling?" Adam asked Grace.

"I'm tired, but I feel relieved. I can relax now that she's here safely."

Her mother suddenly appeared with two cups of coffee and placed them down on the table close to them. "Enjoy the peace while you can because when they get older they're a lot more work."

"*Denke, Mamm*, I'll remember that." She stared down at her baby who was sleeping soundly.

"I better go and see what Marlene's doing in the kitchen."

With Mrs. Byler out of the room, Adam shifted closer to Grace. "There's something I've been meaning to tell you for a while, but the timing never seems right."

"What is it?"

Right at that moment, Matthew ran into the living room. "Has anyone seen Marlene? Did she come in here?"

"*Nee*, we haven't seen her," Grace said while Adam shook his head. "What's wrong?"

"She's run off. She's upset. Can you help me find her, Adam?"

The two men rushed out of the house. Joy opened her eyes and looked around.

AN HOUR LATER, Matthew came home with his arm around Marlene, and Adam wasn't with them. Grace was sitting in the living room and neither of them looked at her when they walked past to head up the stairs.

Grace's mother sat down beside her. "What's wrong with her, do you think?"

"I think it's all the fuss about Joy. Marlene desperately wants to have one of her own. It can't be easy for her."

Grace's mother screwed up her face as though the reason was silly.

"You have to think how she feels, *Mamm*. She longs for something for so long and it's always out of reach, and then I come along and have one without trying."

Her mother leaned back and raised her eyebrows. "Well, you certainly did something, Grace."

"You know what I mean. I wasn't desperate to have one, but she is. She's thinking it's not fair, that's how she feels. She feels *Gott* is not listening to her."

"That's ridiculous."

"Is it?" Grace asked. "I don't think it is. That's how she feels, and even if you'd react differently you can't deny her feelings because they're her feelings."

"She should be enjoying these years before the *bopplis* come along."

"Just be a little nicer to her, *Mamm*. Go easy on her these next few weeks."

Her mother looked horrified. "I'm always nice to Marlene, and we've grown closer since we've been running the market stall."

"She feels like a bit of an outsider."

"Does she?"

Grace nodded.

Mrs. Byler looked thoughtful. "I'll try to be a little more sensitive."

"That would be good." Grace paused. "I wonder why Adam didn't come back with them."

"Why would he? He probably didn't want to make you tired. New *mudders* can get very tired. Sarah would've told him that."

Grace didn't want to tell her mother that Adam was just about to tell her something.

"Now that Marlene's sulking up in her room, I suppose I'm left to do all the breakfast cleanup alone. And she's making Matthew late for work."

"*Mamm!*"

Her mother frowned. "I wasn't being mean."

"That's their concern. If they were living by themselves somewhere other than here, you wouldn't know they were arguing or that Matthew was going to be late. You need to keep out of things a bit."

She took a deep breath. "I suppose you're right."

"I can help you in the kitchen."

"*Nee*, it won't take me long and then I'll sit out here and hold Joy. I haven't had much of a chance yet."

Grace knew she had no choice but to wait until Adam came back. She couldn't go and visit him, not with the baby, and especially when she wasn't sure what he'd wanted to say. When she'd first arrived home, she'd thought they might have had a chance to rekindle their relationship. Was that still a possibility?

Matthew interrupted her thoughts when he came bounding down the stairs by himself.

Grace waved him over and whispered, "How's Marlene?"

"She's upset about the usual thing. I'm worried about her, but I'm late for work."

"Where had she gone?"

"She was just walking down the road when we

found her." He leaned in and whispered, "She suffers from depression and when she ran out like that I feared the worst."

"Thanks for letting me know. Have you only just found this out?"

He shook his head. "She's been bad before, but not this bad."

"I'll keep an eye on her."

"Thank you, Grace," whispered Matthew, as he turned to race out the door.

Grace's father was always the first to leave every morning. Now, the three women and the baby were the only ones in the house.

Grace smelled something strange and looked down at her baby. "Again? Really? *Mamm!*"

Her mother raced into the living room. "Another cup of *kaffe*?"

"How much do you want to spoil me?"

She folded her arms. "Soiled diaper?"

Grace laughed. "How did you know?"

Grace's mother shook her head while she walked over to pick Joy up. "I was wondering how long it'd take before I was changing diapers."

"I was changing them all night; she woke up about three times. For a small baby, I can't believe what comes out of her."

Grace's mother laughed. "I'll take her upstairs and change her. We really should leave some diapers downstairs so we don't have to keep going up and down."

CHAPTER 17

And God shall wipe away all tears from their eyes; and there shall be no more death, neither sorrow, nor crying, neither shall there be any more pain: for the former things are passed away.
Revelation 21:4

A WEEK LATER, Marlene was looking after Joy while Grace took some much needed time alone. She headed down to the creek where she used to go as a child. The more Marlene had helped look after Joy, the more Marlene's mood had improved.

Grace sat on the creek's edge thinking about her life and wondering if she should look for a job. Sure she could smell rain, she looked up at the gray sky. She saw dark rain clouds floating overhead and decided to set off home. When her house came into view, she also saw Adam walking towards her. He waved a hand in the air and she waved back.

"I was just looking for you and they told me you'd gone for a walk."

"*Jah*. I just went to the creek. It's so nice and peaceful there and Marlene loves looking after Joy. I thought I'd give them some aunty-niece time."

"Can I walk with you? I haven't been down to the creek in a while."

Grace looked up at the sky. "Do you think the rain will hold off?"

"I think so," he said. "I'm sorry I didn't come back and finish the conversation that we started days ago."

"It's all right. I think I know what you were going to say, anyway."

"Is it that obvious?" he chuckled.

"Marlene told me about you and Ida. You don't have to say any more."

"Me and Ida?" he looked confused. "Wait a minute, Grace. You've got things wrong."

Grace's heart pumped faster. She knew he liked her and she was teasing him. He took hold of her arm and turned her to face him.

"Grace Byler."

"It's actually Grace Stevens."

"Grace Stevens, I wonder if I might – if you might allow me to take you out for a date."

Grace giggled. "I've never heard you use the word 'date' before."

"It's a word that means you and I will make a time to go somewhere and do something together. What do you say?"

"I say *jah*. I'd like that."

"Of course, you'd have to bring Joy along as our chaperone."

"I'd have to. I can't be away from her for too long when she's this young. I'm missing her already just going on this walk."

Adam was silent for a moment. "I'm sorry, Grace. I lied to you."

At that moment, her heart sank; she couldn't cope with another man who lied. "When?"

"Just then, when I said I wanted to ask you on a date. I don't have to date you or spend any more time with you to know that you're the woman I want to marry." He smiled at her.

She put her hands on her cheeks and gave a nervous giggle.

"Will you marry me, Grace Stevens?"

"*Jah*, Adam. I will marry you."

He pulled her into his arms, lifted her up and swung her around in a circle. He placed her down. "I'm sorry, did I hurt you?"

She laughed. "*Nee*, not at all."

"Shall we go and tell your parents the good news, or shall we keep it to ourselves for the moment?"

"I think we should tell them. I've never been able to keep secrets."

"You kept Marlene's secret very well – the secret that she wrecked my buggy and you didn't. *Nee*, I won't talk about that and ruin our happiness in case you're still angry with me for all the chores I had you do." He grabbed her hand. "Let's go and sit down by the creek like we used to when we were young."

Hand in hand they walked down to the creek. "It's too cold to sit down, so lean against me." He put his arm around her shoulders and pulled her in close to him. He pointed to the tree nearby. "Did you notice our initials are still there?"

She looked over at the tree and recalled the day she stood beside him while he carved the letters into the tree with a penknife. It seemed like a lifetime ago. Now Grace had the man she'd always wanted and she'd been blessed with a baby.

Grace nestled her head into his shoulder while they looked at the icy, half-frozen-over creek. He tilted his head to rest it on top of hers. She appreciated the way he was holding her so tenderly, and she made a mental imprint of that moment so she could remember it forever.

He made the moment more special by whispering, "I'll make you so happy you'll never remember all the horrible things you suffered in your first marriage."

She knew it was true. She'd always known what a good man Adam was. If Marlene hadn't interfered all those years ago, she wouldn't have had baby Joy. Maybe her mother was right about God's timing.

"What are you thinking about, Grace?"

"I'm thinking that we've got Marlene to thank for Joy. If she hadn't told you those lies all those years ago, we might have married back then. I wouldn't have appreciated you as much as I do now, and there'd be no Joy."

"That's true, although her intentions weren't exactly kind. But I guess that even though she had mean intentions for keeping us apart, if I'd married you back then, I wouldn't have known how hard it was to find a woman like you."

Peace flooded through Grace's body, and she wished that the moment would last forever.

"You're an amazing woman. You've gone through such hard times, but they haven't pulled you down, or made you turn from *Gott*. The hard times made you see that *Gott* is the only way."

Grace giggled. "I took a long winding road to get there, but I think my life is finally heading in the right direction."

"Our life – it's our life now. Or will be, as soon as I can talk the bishop into marrying us. We've both been baptized, so there's nothing to stand in our way."

Droplets of rain fell on Grace's head. She tilted her face to the sky. "We should head back."

"I want to stay out here with you a little longer. Just you and me."

As the rain fell, they huddled together under Adam's coat.

"If I don't go back now, they'll be worried about me," Grace said after a few minutes.

"Let's go and share our good news, but I need to tell you something."

"Go on."

"I was scared to let you in. I've always felt alone, and then my parents died and it was just me. I was fearful of getting close to you and then losing you again."

"You won't lose me."

Adam looked up over the water. "It's just a fear. I struggled for a while and wondered if it might be better not to have you at all than to have you and then lose you." He looked into her eyes. "Do you have any idea of what I'm trying to say?"

"Is that why you let me carry on thinking you thought I'd crashed the buggy?"

"That was the day we were going to spend together and I let fear overtake me. I was fearful that you might leave again and I didn't want to go through the pain of losing you a second time. I was going to make some excuse and cancel our plans, but the buggy gave me the perfect escape."

Grace slapped him on his chest. "You let me do all that work in your *haus*."

He laughed. "Don't make me feel worse than I already do. Anyway, it's our *haus*. Yours, Joy's, and mine."

"I hope you know now that I'll never leave again?"

"I do. And when we're married do you think you'll change Joy's last name?"

Grace nodded. "I think that's a good idea. Joy and I are on a journey, and now our journey is with you, so it's only right that we have your last name."

Adam shook his head. "I've got no idea what you're talking about, but I'm glad you've agreed. I want us to be a proper *familye*."

IT WAS two months later when Adam and Grace were sitting at their wedding table as man and wife that Grace noticed Marlene crying. She hadn't seen her cry for a long time so she left Adam and went over to talk to her.

"What's wrong, Marlene?"

"I feel so bad. I nearly ruined things for you with Adam twice. Not once, but twice."

"That doesn't matter now. We're married. This is a time for celebration, not tears."

"It's your day, Grace. It's your special time and I can't ruin it."

Grace frowned. "How would you ruin it?"

Marlene's face scrunched up and tears flowed down her face.

"Stop it! You must tell me. How would you ruin it?" Dark thoughts flashed through her mind. Was Jeremy alive and now she was a bigamist? Was Adam already secretly married? Or did Adam already have a child that no one knew about?

"I can't tell you and ruin your day."

"You must; you must tell me now."

Marlene's bottom lip quivered, and she whispered, "I'm pregnant. I found out this morning, but I didn't want to tell anyone. It's your day. I haven't even told Matthew."

Grace hugged her. "You silly thing. That's *wunderbaar* news. You had me thinking something bad. There's Matthew over there, why don't you take him away in a corner somewhere and tell him?"

Marlene sniffed. "You don't mind me telling people on your special day?"

"Mind? I don't know why you would ever think that I would."

Marlene looked toward Matthew. "I think I'll go tell him now, then."

"I think you should. He's looking at us now and he seems quite concerned."

Marlene gave a little giggle and wiped her eyes before she threw her arms around Grace. "*Denke* for being such a *gut* friend to me. You're more than a friend, you're like a *schweschder,* and not just a *schweschder*-in-law."

Before Grace could say anything, Marlene was hurrying toward Matthew.

Grace sighed and looked over at Adam. Less than a

year ago, she'd had the worst life possible. Jeremy had abused her during their four-year marriage, and then he died. She was left with no money and nothing to her name. The only thing she had was her family and God.

A Scripture she'd heard once was *'all things work together for good.'* Now she knew that it mean that out of bad things, good things can come.

And we know that all things work together for good to them that love God,
to them who are the called according to his purpose.
Romans 8:28

Thank you for reading The Pregnant Amish Widow.

www.SamanthaPriceAuthor.com

THE NEXT BOOK IN THE SERIES

Book 3
Amish Widow's Faith

Emily is a hopeless romantic who loves playing matchmaker. Her latest project is finding a new husband for her recently widowed sister, Deborah. But Deborah is still grieving her late husband and is pregnant with his child, so she's not interested. Emily goes ahead with her plan anyway, but things get complicated when a stranger comes to town.

EXPECTANT AMISH WIDOWS

Book 1 Amish Widow's Hope

Book 2 The Pregnant Amish Widow

Book 3 Amish Widow's Faith

Book 4 Their Son's Amish Baby

Book 5 Amish Widow's Proposal

Book 6 The Pregnant Amish Nanny

Book 7 A Pregnant Widow's Amish Vacation

Book 8 The Amish Firefighter's Widow

Book 9 Amish Widow's Secret

ALL SAMANTHA PRICE'S SERIES

Amish Maids Trilogy
A 3 book Amish romance series of novels featuring 5 friends finding love.

Amish Love Blooms
A 6 book Amish romance series of novels about four sisters and their cousins.

Amish Misfits
A series of 7 stand-alone books about people who have never fitted in.

The Amish Bonnet Sisters
To date there are 28 books in this continuing family saga. My most popular and best-selling series.

Amish Women of Pleasant Valley

An 8 book Amish romance series with the same characters. This has been one of my most popular series.

Ettie Smith Amish Mysteries
An ongoing cozy mystery series with octogenarian sleuths. Popular with lovers of mysteries such as Miss Marple or Murder She Wrote.

Amish Secret Widows' Society
A ten novella mystery/romance series - a prequel to the Ettie Smith Amish Mysteries.

Expectant Amish Widows
A stand-alone Amish romance series of 19 books.

Seven Amish Bachelors
A 7 book Amish Romance series following the Fuller brothers' journey to finding love.

Amish Foster Girls
A 4 book Amish romance series with the same characters who have been fostered to an Amish family.

Amish Brides
An Amish historical romance. 5 book series with the same characters who have arrived in America to start their new life.

Amish Romance Secrets

The first series I ever wrote. 6 novellas following the same characters.

Amish Christmas Books
Each year I write an Amish Christmas stand-alone romance novel.

Amish Twin Hearts
A 4 book Amish Romance featuring twins and their friends.

Amish Wedding Season
The second series I wrote. It has the same characters throughout the 5 books.

Gretel Koch Jewel Thief
A clean 5 book suspense/mystery series about a jewel thief who has agreed to consult with the FBI.

Made in the USA
Las Vegas, NV
16 October 2022